"You would seem to derive from a most remarkable society. You fear the dark, yet it challenges and exalts you. You fear women; you are made uneasy by the female body—still the concept of femininity tantalizes you. You respond positively to martial tactics, heroic encounters, weapons and uniforms; on the other hand you abhor violence and pain. Your other reactions are equally contradictory. The data have been fed into an integrator together with the other background material.

"In my opinion, Master Pardero, or whatever your name, you are a Rhune from the Rhune Realms, east of Port Mar on the North Continent of Marune, Alastor 933."

DM·MR

MARUNE: *Alastor 933*

JACK VANCE

DAW BOOKS, INC.
DONALD A. WOLLHEIM, PUBLISHER

1633 Broadway, New York, NY 10019

Cover art by David B. Mattingly.

first DAW printing, january 1981

1 2 3 4 5 6 7 8 9

MARUNE: Alastor 933

Jack Vance

Alastor Cluster, a node of thirty thousand live stars, uncounted dead hulks, and vast quantities of interstellar detritus, clung to the inner rim of the galaxy with the Unfortunate Waste before, the Nonestic Gulf beyond and the Gaean Reach a sparkling haze to the side. For the spacetraveler, no matter which his angle of approach, a remarkable spectacle was presented: constellations blazing white, blue, and red; curtains of luminous stuff, broken here, obscured there, by black storms of dust; starstreams wandering in and out; whorls and spatters of phosphorescent gas.

Should Alastor Cluster be considered a segment of the Gaean Reach? The folk of the Cluster, some four or five trillion of them on more than three thousand worlds, seldom reflected upon the matter, and indeed considered themselves neither Gaean nor Alastrid. The typical inhabitant, when asked as to his origin, might perhaps cite his native world or, more usually, his local district, as if this place were so extraordinary, so special and widely famed that its reputation hung on every tongue of the galaxy.

Parochialism dissolved before the glory of the Connatic, who ruled Alastor Cluster from his palace on the world Numenes. The current Connatic, Oman Ursht, sixteenth of the Idite dynasty, often pondered the quirk of fate which had appointed him to his singular condition, only to smile at his own irrationality: no matter who occupied the position, that person would frame for himself the same marveling question.

The inhabited planets of the Cluster had little in common except their lack of uniformity. They were large and small, dank and dry, benign and perilous, populous and empty: no two alike. Some manifested tall mountains, blue seas, bright skies; on others clouds hung forever above the moors, and no variety existed except the alternation of night and day. Such a world, in fact, was Bruse-Tansel, Alastor 1102, with a population of two hundred thousand, settled for the most part in the neighborhood of Lake Vain, where they worked principally at the dyeing of fabrics. Four spaceports served Bruse-Tansel, the most important being that facility located at Carfaunge.

Chapter 1

★ ★ ★

The Respectable Mergan had achieved his post, Superintendent at the Carfaunge Spaceport, largely because the position demanded a tolerance for unalterable routine. Mergan not only tolerated routine; he depended upon it. He would have opposed the cessation of such nuisances at the morning rains, the glass lizards with their squeaks and clicks, the walking slimes which daily invaded the area, because then he would have been required to change established procedure.

On the morning of a day he would later identify as tenth Mariel Gaean* he arrived as usual at his office. Almost before he had settled behind his desk, the night porter appeared with a blank-faced young man in a nondescript gray suit. Mergan uttered a wordless grumble; he had no taste for problems at any time, least of all before he had composed himself for the day. The situation at the very least promised a disruption of routine. At last he muttered: "Well, Dinster, what do you have here?"

Dinster, in a piping over-loud voice, called out, "Sorry to bother you, sir, but what shall we do with this gentleman? He seems to be ill."

* Numerous systems of chronometry create confusion across Alastor Cluster and the Gaean Reach, despite attempts at reform. In any given locality, at least three systems of reckoning are in daily use: scientific chronometry, based upon the orbital frequency of the K-state hydrogen electron; astronomic time—'Gaean Standard Time'—which provides synchronism across the human universe; and local time.

"Find him a doctor," growled Mergan. "Don't bring him here. I can't help him."

"It's not that kind of illness, sir. More mental, if you get my meaning."

"Your meaning escapes me," said Mergan. "Why not just tell me what's wrong?"

Dinster politely indicated his charge. "When I came on duty he was sitting in the waiting room and he's been there since. He hardly speaks; he doesn't know his name, nor anything about himself."

Mergan inspected the young man with some faint awakening of interest. "Hello, sir," he barked. "What's the trouble?"

The young man shifted his gaze from the window to Mergan, but offered no response. Mergan gradually allowed himself to become perplexed. Why had the young man's gold-brown hair been hacked short, as if by swift savage strokes of a scissors? And the garments: clearly a size too large for the spare frame!

"Speak!" commanded Mergan. "Can you hear? Tell me your name!"

The young man put on a thoughtful expression but remained silent.

"A vagabond of some sort," Mergan declared. "He probably wandered up from the dye-works. Send him off again down the road."

Dinster shook his head. "This lad's no vagabond. Look at his hands."

Mergan reluctantly followed Dinster's suggestion. The hands were strong and well kept and showed evidence neither of toil nor submersion in dye. The man's features were firm and even; the poise of his head suggested status. Mergan, who preferred to ignore the circumstances of his own birth, felt an uncomfortable tingle of deference and corresponding resentment. Again he barked at the young man: "Who are you? What is your name?"

"I don't know." The voice was slow and labored, and colored with an accent Mergan failed to recognize.

"Where is your home?"

"I don't know."

Mergan became unreasonably sarcastic. "Do you know anything?"

Dinster ventured an opinion. "Looks to me, sir, as if he came aboard one of yesterday's ships."

Mergan asked the young man: "What ship did you arrive on? Do you have friends here?"

The young man fixed him with a brooding dark-gray gaze, and Mergan became uncomfortable. He turned to Dinster. "Does he carry papers? Or money?"

Dinster muttered to the young man: "Excuse me, sir." Gingerly he groped through the pockets of the rumpled gray suit. "I can't find anything here, sir."

"What about ticket stubs, or vouchers, or tokens?"

"Nothing at all, sir."

"It's what they call amnesia," said Mergan. He picked up a pamphlet and glanced down a list. "Six ships in yesterday. He might have arrived on any of them." Mergan touched a button. A voice said: "Prosidine, arrival gate."

Mergan described the amnesiac. "Do you know anything about him? He arrived sometime yesterday."

"Yesterday was more than busy; I didn't take time to notice anything."

"Make inquiries of your people and notify me."

Mergan thought a moment, then called the Carfaunge hospital. He was connected to the Director of Admissions, who listened patiently enough, but made no constructive proposals. "We have no facilities here for such cases. He has no money, you say? Definitely not, then."

"What shall I do with him? He can't stay here!"

"Consult the police; they'll know what to do."

Mergan called the police, and presently an official

arrived in a police van, and the amnesiac was led away.

At the Hall of Inquiry, Detective Squil attempted interrogation, without success. The police doctor experimented with hypnotism, and finally threw up his hands. "A most stubborn condition; I have seen three previous cases, but nothing like this."

"What causes it?"

"Autosuggestion, occasioned by emotional stress. This is most usual. But here"—he waved toward the uncomprehending amnesiac—"my instruments show no psychic charge of any kind. He has no emotions, and I have no leverage."

Detective Squil, a reasonable man, asked: "What can he do to help himself? He is obviously no ruffian."

"He should take himself to the Connatic's Hospital on Numenes."

Detective Squil laughed. "All very well. Who pays his fare?"

"The superintendent at the spaceport should be able to arrange passage, or so I should think."

Squil made a dubious sound but turned to his telephone. As he expected, the Respectable Mergan, having transferred responsibility to the police, wanted no further part of the situation. "The regulations are most explicit," said Mergan. "I certainly cannot do as you suggest."

"We can't keep him here at the station."

"He appears able-bodied; let him earn his fare, which after all is not exorbitant."

"Easier said than done, what with his disability."

"What generally happens to indigents?"

"You know as well as I do; they're sent out to Gaswin. But this man is mentally ill; he's not an indigent."

"I can't argue that, because I don't know. At least I've pointed out a course of action."

"What is the fare to Numenes?"

"Third class by Prydania Line: two hundred and twelve ozols."

Squil terminated the call. He swung about to face the amnesiac. "Do you understand what I say to you?"

The answer came in a clear voice. "Yes."

"You are ill. You have lost your memory. Do you realize this?"

There was a pause of ten seconds. Squil wondered if any response was forthcoming. Then, haltingly: "You have told me so."

"We will send you to a place where you can work and earn money. Do you know how to work?"

"No."

"Well, anyway, you need money: two hundred and twelve ozols. On Gaswin Moor you will earn three and a half ozols a day. In two or three months you will have earned enough money to take you to the Connatic's Hospital on Numenes, where you will be cured of your illness. Do you understand all this?"

The amnesiac reflected a moment, but made no response.

Squil rose to his feet. "Gaswin will be a good place for you, and perhaps your memory will return." He dubiously considered the amnesiac's blond-brown hair, which for mysterious reasons, someone had rudely cut short. "Do you have an enemy? Is there someone who does not like you?"

"I don't know. I can't remember any such person."

"What is your name?" shouted Squil, hoping to surprise that part of the brain which was withholding information.

The amnesiac's gray eyes narrowed slightly. "I don't know."

"Well, we have to find a name for you. Do you play hussade?"

"No."

"Think of that! A strong agile fellow like yourself! Still, we'll call you Pardero, after the great strike forward of the Schaide Thunderstones. So now, when someone calls out 'Pardero' you must respond. Is this understood?"

"Yes."

"Very well, and now you'll be on your way to Gaswin. The sooner you begin your work, the sooner you'll arrive on Numenes. I'll speak with the director; he's a good chap and he'll see to your welfare."

Pardero, as his name now would be, sat uncertainly. Squil took pity on him. "It won't be so bad. Agreed, there are tough nuts at the work camp, but do you know how to handle them? You must be just a bit tougher than they are. Still, don't attract the attention of the disciplinary officer. You seem a decent fellow; I'll put in a word for you, and keep an eye on your progress. One bit of advice—no, two. First: never try to cheat on your work quota. The officials know all the tricks; they can smell out the sluggards as a kribbat smells out carrion. Second, do not gamble! Do you know what the word 'gamble' means?"

"No."

"It means to risk your money on games or wagers. Never be tempted or inveigled! Leave your money in the camp account! I advise you to form no friendships! Aside from yourself, there is only riff-raff at the camp. I wish you well. If you find trouble, call for Detective Squil. Can you remember that name?"

"Detective Squil."

"Good." Squil led the amnesiac out to a dock and put him aboard the daily transport to Gaswin. "A final word of advice! Confide in no one! Your name is Pardero; aside from this, keep your problems to yourself! Do you understand?"

"Yes."

"Good luck!"

The transport flew low under the overcast, close above the mottled black and purple moors, and presently landed beside a cluster of concrete buildings: the Gaswin Work Camp.

At the personnel office Pardero underwent entry formalities, facilitated by Squil's notification to the camp director. He was assigned a cubicle in a dormitory block, fitted with work boots and gloves, and issued a copy of camp regulations, which he studied without comprehension. On the next morning, he was detailed into a work party and sent out to harvest pods from colucoid creeper, the source of a peculiarly rich red dye.

Pardero gathered his quota without difficulty. Among the taciturn group of indigents his deficiency went unnoticed.

He ate his evening meal in silence, ignoring the presence of his fellows, who at last had begun to sense that all was not well with Pardero.

The sun sank behind the clouds; a dismal twilight fell across the moors. Pardero sat to the side of the recreation hall, watching a comic melodrama on the holovision screen. He listened intently to the dialogue; each word seemed to find an instantly receptive niche inside his brain with a semantic concept ready at hand. His vocabulary grew and the range of his mental processes expanded. When the program was over he sat brooding, at last aware of his condition. He went to look into the mirror over the washbasin; the face which looked back at him was at once strange and familiar: a somber face with a good expanse of forehead, prominent cheekbones, hollow cheeks, dark gray eyes, a ragged thatch of dark gold hair.

A certain burly rogue named Woane attempted a jocularity. "Look yonder at Pardero! He stands like a man admiring a beautiful work of art!"

Pardero studied the mirror. Who was the man whose eyes stared so intently into his own?

Woane's hoarse murmur came from across the room. "Now he admires his haircut."

The remark amused Woane's friends. Pardero turned his head this way and that, wondering as to the motive behind the assault on his hair. Somewhere, it would seem, he had enemies. He turned slowly away from the mirror and resumed his seat at the side of the room.

The last traces of light left the sky; night had come to Gaswin Camp.

Something jerked deep at the bottom of Pardero's consciousness: a compulsion totally beyond his comprehension. He jumped to his feet. Woane looked around half-truculently, but Pardero's glance slid past him. Woane nevertheless saw or felt something sufficiently eery that his jaw dropped a trifle, and he muttered to his friends. All watched as Pardero crossed to the door and went out into the night.

Pardero stood on the porch. Floodlights cast a wan glow across the compound, now empty and desolate, inhabited only by the wind from the moors. Pardero stepped off the porch into the shadows. With no purpose he walked around the edge of the compound and out upon the moor; the camp became an illuminated island behind him.

Under the overcast, darkness was complete. Pardero felt an enlargement of the soul, an intoxication of power, as if he were an elemental born of the darkness, knowing no fear . . . He stopped short. His legs felt hard and strong; his hands tingled with competence. Gaswin Camp lay a half-mile behind him, the single visible object. Pardero took a deep throbbing breath, and again examined his consciousness, half-hoping, half-fearful of what he might find.

Nothing. Recollection extended to the Carfaunge

spaceport. Events before were like voices remembered from a dream. Why was he here at Gaswin? To earn money. How long must he remain? He had forgotten, or perhaps the words had not registered. Pardero began to feel a suffocating agitation, a claustrophobia of the intellect. He lay down on the moor, beat his forehead, cried out in frustration.

Time passed. Pardero rose to his knees, gained his feet and slowly returned to camp.

A week later Pardero learned of the camp doctor and his function. The next morning, during sick call, he presented himself to the dispensary. A dozen men sat on the benches while the doctor, a young man fresh from medical school, summoned them forward, one at a time. The complaints, real, imaginary, or contrived, were usually related to the work: backache, allergic reaction, congestion of the lungs, an infected lychbug sting. The doctor, young in years but already old in guile, sorted out the real from the fictitious, prescribing remedies for the first and irritant salves or vile-flavored medicines for the second.

Pardero was signaled to the desk and the doctor looked him up and down. "What's wrong with you?"

"I can't remember anything."

"Indeed." The doctor leaned back in his chair. "What is your name?"

"I don't know. Here at the camp they call me Pardero. Can you help me?"

"Probably not. Go back to the bench and let me finish up the sick call; it'll be just a few minutes."

The doctor dealt with his remaining patients and returned to Pardero. "Tell me how far back you remember."

"I arrived at Carfaunge. I remember a spaceship. I remember the depot—but nothing before."

"Nothing whatever?"

"Nothing."

"Do you remember things you like, or dislike? Are you afraid of anything?"

"No."

"Amnesia typically derives from a subconscious intent to block out intolerable memories."

Pardero gave his head a dubious shake. "I don't think this is likely."

The doctor, both intrigued and bemused, uttered an uneasy half-embarrassed laugh. "Since you can't remember the circumstances, you aren't in a position to judge."

"I suppose that's true . . . Could something be wrong with my brain?"

"You mean physical damage? Do you have headaches or head pains? Any sensation of numbness or pressure?"

"No."

"Well, it's hardly likely a tumor would cause general amnesia in any event . . . Let me check my references . . ." He read for a few moments. "I could try hypnotherapy or shock. Candidly, I don't think I'd do you any good. Amnesia generally cures itself if left alone."

"I don't think I can cure myself. Something lies on my brain like a blanket. It suffocates me. I can't tear it loose. Can't you help me?"

There was a simplicity to Pardero's manner which appealed to the doctor. He also sensed strangeness: tragedy and drama beyond his conjecture.

"I would help you if I could," said the doctor. "With all my soul I would help you. But I wouldn't know what I should be doing. I'm not qualified to experiment on you."

"The police officer told me to go to the Connatic's Hospital on Numenes."

"Yes, of course. This is best for you; I was about to suggest it myself."

"Where is Numenes? How do I go there?"

"You must go by starship. The fare is a little over two hundred ozols. That is what I have been told. You earn three and a half ozols a day—more if you exceed your quota. When you have two hundred and fifty ozols, go to Numenes. That is my best advice."

Chapter 2

★ ★ ★

Pardero worked with single-minded energy. Without fail he collected a half measure over his quota, and sometimes a total of two measures, which first excited jocular comment among his fellow workers, then sardonic sneers, and finally a cold, if covert, hostility. To compound his offenses Pardero refused to participate in the social activities of the camp, except to sit staring into the holovision screen, and thereby was credited with assumptions of superiority, which was indeed the case. He spent nothing at the commissary; despite all persuasions he refused to gamble, although occasionally he watched the games with a grim smile, which made certain of the players uneasy. Twice his locker was ransacked by someone who hoped to avail himself of Pardero's earnings, but Pardero had drawn no money from his account. Woane made one or two half-hearted attempts at intimidation, then decided to chastise the haughty Pardero, but he encountered such ferocious retaliation that he was glad to regain the sanctuary of the mess hall; and thereafter Pardero was strictly ignored.

At no time could Pardero detect any seepage through the barrier between his memory and his conscious mind. Always as he worked he wondered: "What kind of man am I? Where is my home? What do I know? Who are my friends? Who has committed this wrong upon me?" He expended his frustration on the colucoid creeper and became known as a man possessed by an inner demon, to be avoided as carefully as possible.

For his part Pardero banished Gaswin to the most remote corner of his mind; he would take away as few memories as possible. The work he found tolerable; but he resented the name Pardero. To use a stranger's name was like wearing a stranger's clothes—not a fastidious act. Still the name served as well as any other; it was a minor annoyance.

More urgently unpleasant was the lack of privacy. He found detestable the close intimacy of three hundred other men, most especially at mealtimes, when he sat with his eyes fixed on his plate, to avoid the open maws, the mounds of food, the mastication. Impossible to ignore, however, were the belches, grunts, hisses, and sighs of satiety. Surely this was not the life he had known in the past! What then had been his life?

The question produced only blankness, a void without information. Somewhere lived a person who had launched him across the Cluster with his hair hacked short and as denuded of identification as an egg. Sometimes when he pondered this enemy he seemed to hear wisps of possibly imaginary sound—echoes of what might have been laughter, but when he poised his head to listen, the pulsations ceased.

The onset of darkness continued to trouble him. Often he felt urges to go forth into the dark—an impulse which he resisted, partly from fatigue, partly from a dread of abnormality. He reported his nocturnal restlessness to the camp doctor, who agreed that the tendency should be discouraged, at least until the source was known. The doctor commended Pardero for his industry, and advised the accumulation of at least two hundred and seventy-five ozols before departure, to allow for incidental expenses.

When Pardero's account reached two hundred and seventy-five ozols, he claimed his money from the bursar, and now, no longer an indigent, he was free to pursue his own destiny. He took a rather mournful leave of the doctor, whom he had come to like and respect, and boarded the transport for Carfaunge. He left Gaswin with a twinge of regret. He had known little pleasure here; still the place had given him refuge. He barely remembered Carfaunge, and the spaceport was no more than the recollection of a dream.

He saw nothing of Superintendent Mergan, but was recognized by Dinster the night porter, just coming on duty.

The *Ectobant* of the Prydania Line took Pardero to Baruilla, on Deulle, Alastor 2121, where he transferred to the *Lusimar* of the Gaean Trunk Line, and so was conveyed to Calypso Junction on Imber, and thence by the *Wispen Argent* to Numenes.

Pardero enjoyed the voyage: the multifarious sensations, incidents, and vistas amazed him. He had not imagined the variety of the Cluster: the comings and goings, the flux of faces, the gowns, robes, hats, ornaments, and bijouterie; the colors and lights and strains of strange music; the babble of voices; haunting glimpses of beautiful girls; drama, excitement, pathos; objects, faces, sounds, surprises. Could he have known all this and forgotten?

So far Pardero had not indulged in self-pity and his enemy had seemed a baleful abstraction. But how great and how callous the crime which had been performed upon him! He had been isolated from home, friends, sympathy, security; he had been rendered a neuter; his personality had been murdered.

Murder!

The word chilled his blood; he squirmed and winced. And from somewhere, from far distant, came the ghost of a sound: gusts of mocking laughter.

Approaching Numenes, the *Wispen Argent* first passed by Blazon, the next world out in orbit, to be cleared for landing by the Whelm—a precaution to minimize the danger of an attack from space upon the Connatic's Palace. Having secured clearance, the *Wispen Argent* proceeded; Numenes slowly expanded.

At a distance of about three thousand miles that peculiar referential displacement occurred; instead of hanging off to the side, a destination across the void, Numenes became the world below, upon which the *Wispen Argent* descended—a brilliant panorama of white clouds, blue air, sparkling seas.

The Central Spaceport at Commarice occupied an area three miles in diameter, surrounded by a fringe of the tall jacinth palms and the usual spaceport offices, built in that low airy style also typical of Numenes.

Alighting from the *Wispen Argent,* Pardero rode a slideway to the terminal, where he sought information regarding the Connatic's Hospital. He was referred first to the Traveler's Aid Station, then to an office at the side of the terminal, where he was presented to a tall spare woman of indeterminate age in a white and blue uniform. She gave Pardero a laconic greeting. "I am Matron Gundal. I understand that you wish to be admitted to the Connatic's Hospital?"

"Yes."

Matron Gundal touched buttons, evidently to activate a recording mechanism. "Your name?"

"I am called Pardero. I do not know my true name."

Matron Gundal made no comment. "Place of origin?"

"I don't know."

"Your complaint?"

"Amnesia."

Matron Gundal gave him a noncommittal inspection, which perhaps indicated interest. "What about your physical health?"

"It seems to be good."

"An orderly will conduct you to the hospital." Matron Gundal raised her voice. "Ariel."

A blond young woman entered the room, her uniform somewhat at discord with her sunny good looks. Matron Gundal gave her directions: "Please conduct this gentleman to the Connatic's Hospital." To Pardero: "Have you luggage?"

"No."

"I wish you a quick recovery."

The orderly smiled politely at Pardero. "This way, please."

An aircab slid them northward across the blue and green landscape of Flor Solana, with Ariel maintaining an easy flow of conversation. "Have you visited Numenes before?"

"I don't know; I don't remember anything earlier than the last two or three months."

"Oh, I'm sorry to hear this!" said Ariel in confusion. "Well, in case you don't know, there are no real continents here on Numenes, just islands. Everybody who lives here owns a boat."

"That seems very pleasant."

Ariel gingerly touched upon Pardero's disability, watching sidelong to see if he evinced sensitivity or discomfort. "What a strange sensation not to know yourself! How does it feel?"

Pardero considered a moment. "Well—it doesn't hurt."

"I'm relieved to hear that! Think: you might be almost anyone—perhaps rich and important!"

"More likely I'm someone very ordinary: a road-mender, or a wandering dog-barber."

"I'm sure not!" declared Ariel. "You seem—well . . ." she hesitated, then continued with a half-embarrassed laugh "—a very confident and intelligent person."

"I hope you are right." Pardero looked at her and sighed, wistful that her fresh blond charm must so soon pass from his life. "What will they do with me?"

"Nothing alarming. Your case will be studied by very clever persons using the most elaborate mechanisms. Almost certainly you will be cured."

Pardero felt a pang of uneasiness. "It's quite a gamble. I might easily be someone I don't want to be."

Ariel could not restrain a grin. "As I understand it, this is the reason persons become amnesiac in the first place."

Pardero made a glum sound. "Aren't you alarmed, riding with a man who likely is a shameful criminal?"

"I'm paid to be brave. I escort persons much more alarming than you."

Pardero looked out across Flor Solana Island. Ahead he saw a pavilion constructed of pale ribs and translucent panels, whose complexity was obscured behind jacinth palms and cinniborines.

As the aircab approached, six domes became evident, with wings radiating in six directions. Pardero asked: "Is this the hospital?"

"The hospital is everything you see. The Hexad is the computative center. The smaller buildings are laboratories and surgeries. Patients are housed in the wings. That will be your home until you are restored to health."

Pardero asked diffidently: "And what of you? Will I see you again?"

Ariel's dimples deepened. "Do you want to?"

Pardero soberly considered the range of his inclinations. "Yes."

Ariel said half-teasingly: "You'll be so preoccupied that you'll forget all about me."

"I never want to forget anything again."

Ariel chewed her lip thoughtfully. "You remember nothing of you past life?"

"Nothing."

"Maybe you have a family: someone who loves you, and children."

"I suppose this is possible . . . Somehow I suspect otherwise."

"Most men seem to suspect otherwise . . . Well, I'll have to think about it."

The aircab landed; the two alighted and walked along a tree-shaded avenue toward the Hexad. Ariel glanced at him sidewise, and perhaps his obvious foreboding excited her compassion. She said in a voice which she intended to be cheerful but impersonal: "I'm out here often and as soon as you've started your treatments I'll come and see you."

Pardero smiled wanly. "I'll look forward to the occasion."

She conducted him to the reception area, and spoke a few words to an official, then took her leave. "Don't forget!" she called over her shoulder, and the impersonality, intentionally or not, was gone from her voice. "I'll see you soon!"

"I am O.T. Kolodin," said a large rather rumpled man with an oversize nose and sparse untidy dark hair. "'O.T.' means 'Ordinary Technician'; just call me Kolodin. You're on my list, so we'll be seeing something of each other. Come along; I'll get you settled."

Pardero bathed, submitted to a physical examination, and was issued a pale blue lightweight suit. Kolodin showed him to his chamber along one of the wings, and the two took a meal on a nearby terrace. Kolodin, not too much older than Pardero but incalculably more sophisticated, took a lively interest in Pardero's condition. "I've never come in contact with such a case before. Fascinating! It's almost a shame to cure you!"

Pardero managed a wry smile. "I have doubts of my own. I'm told that I can't remember because of something I want to forget. I might not like being cured."

"It is a difficult position," Kolodin agreed. "Still, affairs may not be so bad after all." He glanced at his thumbnail, which responded with a set of glowing numbers. "In fifteen minutes we'll meet with M.T. Rady, who will decide upon your therapy."

The two returned to the Hexad. Kolodin ushered Pardero into the office of Master Technician Rady, and a moment later Rady himself appeared: a thin sharp-eyed man of middle age who already seemed to know the data relevant to Pardero's case. He asked: "The spaceship which brought you to Bruse-Tansel: how was it named?"

"I can't remember much about it."

Rady nodded and touched a square of coarse sponge to each of Pardero's shoulders. "This is an inoculation to facilitate a relaxed mind-state . . . Relax back into your chair. Can you fix your mind upon something pleasant?"

The room dimmed; Pardero thought of Ariel. Rady said: "On the wall you will see a pair of designs. I want you to examine them, or if you prefer, you may close your eyes and rest . . . In fact, relax completely, and listen only to my voice; and when I tell you to sleep, then you may sleep."

The designs on the wall pulsed and swam; a soft sound, waxing and waning, seemed to absorb and obliterate all other sounds of the universe. The shapes on the wall had expanded to surround him, and the only reality was himself and his inner mind.

"I don't know." The voice sounded as if it were coming from a distant room, although it was his own voice. Odd. He heard a mumble whose significance he only half-heeded: "What was your father's name?"

"I don't know."

"What was your mother's name?"

"I don't know."

More questions, sometimes casual, sometimes urgent, and always the same response, and finally the cessation of sound.

Pardero awoke in an empty office. Almost immediately Rady returned, to stand looking down at Pardero with a faint smile.

Pardero asked: "What did you learn?"

"Nothing to speak of. How do you feel?"

"Tired."

"Quite normal. For the rest of the day, rest. Don't worry about your condition; somehow we'll get to the bottom of your case."

"Suppose there's nothing there? Suppose I have no memory?"

Rady refused to take the idea seriously. "Every cell in your body has a memory. Your mind stores facts on many levels. For instance you have not forgotten how to speak."

Pardero said dubiously: "When I arrived at Carfaunge, I knew very little. I could not talk. As soon as I heard a word I remembered its meaning and I could use it."

Rady gave a curt nod. "This is the basis of a therapy we might well try."

Pardero hesitated. "I might find my memory and discover myself to be a criminal."

Rady's eyes gleamed. "That is a chance you must

take. The Connatic, after restoring your memory, might then decide to put you to death."

Pardero grimaced. "Does the Connatic ever visit the hospital?"

"Undoubtedly. He goes everywhere."

"What does he look like?"

Rady shrugged. "In his official photographs he seems an important and imposing nobleman, because of his dress and accoutrements. But when he walks abroad, he goes quietly and is never recognized, and this is what he likes best. Four trillion folk inhabit Alastor Cluster, and it is said that the Connatic knows what each of them eats for breakfast."

"In that case," said Pardero, "perhaps I should simply go to ask the Connatic for the facts of my life."

"It might come to that."

The days passed, and then a week, and then two weeks. Rady attempted a dozen stratagems to loosen the blocked linkages in Pardero's mind. He recorded responses to a gamut of stimulations: colors, sounds, odors, tastes, textures; heights and depths; lights and degrees of darkness. On a more complex level he charted Pardero's reactions, overt, physiological, and cephalic, to absurdities and festivals, erotic conditions, cruelties and horrors, the faces of men, women, and children. A computational mechanism assimilated the results of the tests, compared them to known parameters, and synthesized an analog of Pardero's psyche.

Rady, when he finally assessed the results of his tests, found little enlightenment. "Your basic reflexes are ordinary enough; one anomaly is your reaction to darkness, by which you seem to be curiously stimulated. Your social perceptivity seems underdeveloped, for which the amnesia may be to blame. You appear to be assertive rather than retiring; your response to music is minimal and color symbology has little meaning for you—possibly by reason of your amnesia.

Odors stimulate you rather more than I might expect—but to no significant degree." Rady leaned back in his chair. "These tests might easily provoke some sort of conscious response. Have you noticed anything whatever?"

"Nothing."

Rady nodded. "Very well. We will try a new tack. The theoretical basis is this: if your amnesia has resulted from circumstances which you are determined to forget, we can dissolve the amnesia by bringing these events to your conscious attention again. In order to do this, we must learn the nature of the traumatic circumstances. In short we must learn your identity and home environment."

Pardero frowned and looked out the window. Rady watched intently. "You don't care to learn your identity?"

Pardero gave him a crooked smile. "I did not say so."

Rady shrugged. "The choice is yours. You can walk out of here at any time. The Social Service will find you employment and you can start a new life."

Pardero shook his head. "I never could evade the pressure. Perhaps there are people who need me, who now grieve for me."

Rady said only: "Tomorrow we'll start the detective work."

An hour after twilight Pardero met Ariel at a café and reported the events of the day. "Rady admitted bafflement," said Pardero, with something like gloomy satisfaction. "Not in so many words of course. He also said that the only way to learn where I came from was to find out where I lived. In short, he wants to send me home. First we must find home. The detective work starts tomorrow."

Ariel nodded thoughtfully. Tonight she was not her

usual self; in fact, thought Pardero, she seemed strained and preoccupied. He reached out to touch her soft blond hair, but she drew back.

"And then?" she asked.

"Nothing much. He told me that if I were reluctant to proceed, now was the time to make a decision."

"And what did you say?"

"I told him that I had to go on, that perhaps somewhere people searched for me."

Ariel's blue eyes darkened sorrowfully. "I cannot see you anymore, Pardero."

"Oh? Why not?"

"For just the reasons you cited. Amnesiacs always wander away from their homes and then—well, form new attachments. Then their memory returns and the situation ends in tragedy." Ariel rose to her feet. "I'll say good-bye now, before I change my mind." She touched his hand, then walked away from the table. Pardero watched her diminish down the avenue. He made no move to stop her.

Instead of one day, three days passed before O.T. Kolodin sought out Pardero. "Today we visit the Connatic's Palace and explore the Ring of Worlds."

"I'll enjoy the excursion. But why?"

"I've been looking into your past, and it turns out to be a hopeless tangle; or, more properly, a blur of uncertainties."

"I could have told you that myself."

"No doubt, but one must never take anything for granted. The facts, duly certified, are these. Sometime on tenth Mariel Gaean you appeared at Carfaunge Spaceport. This was an unusually busy day and you might have arrived aboard any of six ships of four different transport lines. The previous routes of these ships took them to a total of twenty-eight worlds, any of which might be your place of origin. Nine of these worlds are important junctions and it is possible that you made your voyage by two or even three stages. Amnesia would not be an insuperable objection. Stewards and depot personnel, taking you for a lackwit, would consult your ticket and shift you from ship to ship. In any case the number of worlds, depots, ships, and possible linkages becomes unmanageable. Or at least an inquiry of last resort. First we will visit the Connatic! Though I doubt if he will receive us personally."

"Too bad! I would like to pay my respects."

They rode by aircab across Flor Solana to Moniscq, a town beside the sea, thence under the Ocean of Equatorial Storms by submarine tunnel to Tremone Island. An airbus flew them south, and presently the Connatic's so-called "palace" became visible, appearing first as a fragile shine, an unsubstantial glimmer in the air, which solidified into a tower of stupendous dimensions, standing upon five pylons, footed upon five islands. A thousand feet above the sea the pylons joined and flared, creating a dome of five groins, the underside of the first deck. Above rose the tower, up through the lower air, up through the sunny upper air, through a wisp of cirrus to terminate in the high sunlight. Kolodin asked casually: "Have you such towers on your home world?"*

Pardero glanced at him skeptically. "Are you trying to trick me? If I knew this, I wouldn't be here." He returned to contemplation of the tower. "And where does the Connatic live?"

"He has apartments at the pinnacle. Perhaps he stands up there now, by one of his windows. Again, perhaps not. It is never certain; after all, dissidents, rogues, and rebels are not unknown to Alastor, and precautions are in order. Suppose, for example, that an

* A drab translation of the word *geisling*, which carries warmer and dearer connotations.

assassin were sent to Numenes in the guise of an amnesiac, or perhaps as an amnesiac with horrid instructions latent in his mind."

"I have no weapons," said Pardero. "I am no assassin. The very thought causes me to shudder."

"I must make a note of this. I believe that your psychometry also showed an aversion to murder. Well, if you are an assassin, the plan will not succeed, as I doubt if we shall see the Connatic today."

"Who then will we be seeing?"

"A certain demosophist named Ollave, who has access to the data banks and the collating machinery. Quite possibly we will today learn the name of your home world."

Pardero gave the matter his usual careful consideration. "And then what will happen to me?"

"Well," said Kolodin cautiously, "three options at least are open. You can continue therapy at the hospital, although I fear that Rady is discouraged. You can accept your condition and attempt a new life. You can return to your home world."

Pardero made no comment, and Kolodin delicately forebore to put any further questions.

A slideway conveyed them to the base of the near pylon, from which perspective the tower's proportions could no longer be sensibly discerned, and only the sensation of overwhelming mass and transcendent engineering remained.

The two ascended in an elevator bubble; the sea, the shore, and Tremone Island dropped below.

"The first three decks and the six lower promenades are reserved for the use and pleasure of tourists. Here they may wander for days enjoying simple relaxation or, at choice, exotic entertainments. They may sleep without charge in simple chambers, although luxurious apartments are available at nominal expense. They may dine upon familiar staples or they may test every reputable cuisine of the Cluster and elsewhere, again at minimal cost. Travelers come and go by the millions; such is the Connatic's wish. Now we pass the administrative decks, which house the government agencies and the offices of the Twenty-Four Agents . . . Now we pass the Ring of Worlds, and up to the College of Anthropological Sciences, and here is our destination. Ollave is a man most knowledgeable and if anything can be learned he will learn it."

They stepped forth into a lobby tiled in blue and white. Kolodin spoke the name Ollave toward a black disk, and presently Ollave appeared. He was a man of undistinguished appearance, his face sallow and pensive, with a long thin nose and black hair receding from a narrow forehead. He greeted Kolodin and Pardero in a voice unexpectedly heavy and took them into a sparsely furnished office. Pardero and Kolodin sat in chairs and Ollave settled behind his desk. Ollave addressed Pardero: "As I understand the situation, you remember nothing of your early life."

"This is true."

"I cannot give you your memory," said Ollave, "but if you are native to Alastor Cluster, I should be able to determine your world of origin, perhaps the precise locality of your home district."

"How will you do that?"

Ollave indicated his desk. "I have on record your anthropometry, physiological indices, details as to your somatic chemistry, psychic profile—in fact all the information Technicians Rady and Kolodin have been able to adduce. Perhaps you are aware that residence upon any particular world in any specific society, and participation in any way of life leaves traces, mental and physical. These traces unfortunately are not absolutely specific, and some are too subtle to be reliably measured. For instance, if you are characterized by blood type RC3, it is then unlikely that your home world is Azulias. Your intestinal bacteria furnish clues, as does the musculature of your legs, the chemical composition of your hair, the presence and nature of any body fungus or internal parasite; the pigments of your skin. If you make use of gestures these may be typified. Other social reflexes such as areas and degrees of personal modesty are also indicative, but these require long and patient observation and again may be obscured by the amnesia. Dentition and dental repairs sometimes offer a clue, as does hairstyling. So now: do you understand the process? Those parameters to which we can assign numerical weights are processed in a computer, which will then present us a list of places in descending order of probability.

"We will prepare two other such lists. To those worlds most convenient to Carfaunge Spaceport we will assign probability factors, and we will try to codify your cultural reflexes: a complex undertaking, as the amnesia no doubt has muted much of this data, and you have in the meantime acquired a set of new habits. Still, if you will step into the laboratory, we will try to make a reading."

In the laboratory Ollave sat Pardero in a massive chair, fitted receptors to various parts of his body, and adjusted a battery of contacts to his head. Over Pardero's eyes he placed optical hemispheres and clamped earphones to his ears.

"First we establish your sensitivity to archetypal concepts. Amnesia may well dampen or distort the responses, and according to M.T. Rady yours is an extraordinary case. Still, if the cerebellum only is occluded other areas of the nervous system will provide information. If we get any signals whatever, we will assume that their relative strength has remained constant. The recent overlay we will try to screen out. You are to do nothing, merely sit quiet; attempt neither to feel nor not to feel; your internal faculties will provide us all we want to know." He closed the hemispheres over Pardero's eyes. "First, a set of elemental concepts."

To Pardero's eyes and ears were presented scenes and sounds: a sunlit forest, surf breaking upon a beach, a meadow sprinkled with flowers, a mountain valley roaring to a winter storm; a sunset, a starry night, a view over a calm ocean, a city street, a road winding over placid hills, a spaceship.

"Now another series," came Ollave's voice. Pardero saw a campfire surrounded by shadowy figures, a beautiful nude maiden, a corpse dangling from a gibbet, a warrior in black steel armor galloping on a horse, a parade of harlequins and clowns, a sailboat plunging through the waves, three old ladies sitting on a bench.

"Next, musics."

A series of musical sounds entered Pardero's ears: a pair of chords, several orchestral essays, a fanfare, the music of a harp, a jig, and a merrydown.

"Now faces."

A stern and grizzled man stared at Pardero, a child, a middle-aged woman, a girl, a face twisted into a sneer, a boy laughing, a man in pain, a woman weeping.

"Vehicles."

Pardero saw boats, chariots, landvehicles, aircraft, spaceships.

"The body."

Pardero saw a hand, a face, a tongue, a nose, an abdomen, male and female genital organs, an eye, an open mouth, buttocks, a foot.

"Places."

A cabin beside a lake, a palace of a dozen domes and cupolas in a garden, a wooden hut, an urban tenement, a houseboat, a temple, a laboratory, the mouth of a cave.

"Objects."

A sword, a tree, a coil of rope, a mountain crag, an energy gun, a plow with a shovel and hoe, an official proclamation with a red seal, flowers in a vase, books on a shelf, an open book on a lectern, carpenter's tools, a selection of musical instruments, mathematical adjuncts, a retort, a whip, an engine, an embroidered pillow, a set of maps and charts, draughting instruments and blank paper.

"Abstract symbols."

Patterns appeared before Pardero's vision: combination of lines, geometrical shapes, numbers, linguistic characters, a clenched fist, a pointing finger, a foot with small wings growing from the ankles.

"And finally . . ." Pardero saw himself—from a distance, then close at hand. He looked into his own face.

Ollave removed the apparatus. "The signals were extremely faint but perceptible. We have recorded your psychometrics and now can establish your so-called cultural index."

"What have you learned?"

Ollave gave Pardero a rather queer look. "You reactions are inconsistent, to use an understatement. You would seem to derive from a most remarkable society. You fear the dark, yet it challenges and exalts you. You fear women; you are made uneasy by the female body—still the concept of femininity tantalizes you. You respond positively to martial tactics, heroic encounters, weapons and uniforms; on the other hand you abhor violence and pain. Your other reactions are equally contradictory. The question becomes, do all these strange responses form a pattern, or do they indicate derangement? I will not speculate. The data have been fed into an integrator together with the other material I mentioned. No doubt the report is ready for us."

"I am almost afraid to examine it," murmured Pardero. "I would seem to be unique."

Ollave made no further comment; they returned to the office, where O.T. Kolodin waited patiently. From a register Ollave drew forth a square of white paper.

"Here is our report." In a manner perhaps unconsciously dramatic he studied the printout. "A pattern has appeared." He read the sheet again. "Ah, yes . . . Eighteen localities on five worlds are identified. The probabilities for four of these worlds, with seventeen of the localities, aggregate three percent. The probability for the single locality on the fifth world is rated at eighty-nine percent, which under the circumstances is equivalent to near-certainty. In my opinion, Master Pardero, or whatever your name, you are a Rhune from the Rhune Realms, east of Port Mar on the North Continent of Marune, Alastor 933."

Chapter 3

★ ★ ★

In the blue- and white-tiled lobby Kolodin asked Pardero: "Well—so you are a Rhune. What then? Do you recognize the word?"

"Not at all."

"I suspected not."

Ollave joined them. "Let's go acquaint ourselves with this world of yours. The Ring is directly below; Chamber 933 will be on Leval Five. To the descendor!"

As the bubble dropped them down the levels, Kolodin discoursed upon the Ring of Worlds. "—one of the few areas controlled by entrance permit. Not so in the early days. Anyone might visit his world's chamber and there perform whatever nuisance entered his head, such as writing his name on the wall, or inserting a pin into the globe at the site of his home, or altering the lineage of local nobility, or placing scurrilous reports into the records. As a result we must now declare ourselves."

"Luckily my credentials will facilitate the matter," said Ollave drily.

The formalities accomplished, an attendant took them to that portal numbered 933 and allowed them admittance.

In the center of the chamber a globe ten feet in diameter floated close above the floor, rotating easily to the touch. "And there you see Marune," said Kolodin. "Does it appear familiar? . . . As I expected."

Ollave touched the globe. "A small dense world of no great population. The color gradients represent relief; Marune is a most rugged world. Notice these peaks and chasms! The olive green areas are polar tundra; the smooth blue metal is open water: not a great deal, relatively speaking. Note too these vast equatorial bogs! Certainly there is little habitable land." He touched a button; the globe sparkled with small pink light-points. "There you see the population distribution: Port Mar seems to be the largest city. But feel free to look around the chamber; perhaps you will see something to stimulate your memory."

Pardero moved here and there, studying the exhibits, charts, and cases with only tentative interest. Presently he asked in a rather hollow voice: "How far away is this planet?"

Kolodin took him to a three-dimensional representation of Alastor Cluster. "Here we are on Numenes, beside this yellow star." He touched a button, a red indicator blinked, near the side of the display. "There is Marune, almost at the Cold Edge, in the Fontinella Wisp. Bruse-Tansel is somewhere about there, where those grid lines come together." He moved to another display. "This represents the local environment: a four-star group. Marune is"—he touched a button—

"at the end of the red arrow, orbiting close around the orange dwarf Furad. The green star is Cirse, the blue dwarf is Osmo, the red dwarf if Maddar. A spectacular location for a planet, among such a frolic of stars! Maddar and Cirse swing close around each other; Furad, with Marune keeping its monthly orbit, curves around Osmo; the four stars dance a fine saraband down the Fontinella Wisp."

Then Kolodin read from a placard on the wall. " 'On Marune, day and night do not alternate as is the case with most planets. Instead, there are varying conditions of light, depending upon which sun or suns rule the sky; and these periods are designated by a specific nomenclature. Aud, isp, red rowan, green rowan, and umber are the ordinary gradations. Night occurs at intervals regulated by a complex pattern, on the average about once every thirty days.

" 'Most of Marune is poorly adapted to human habitation and the population is small, divided about equally between agriculturists of the lowland slopes and residents of the several cities, of which Port Mar is by far the most important. East of Port Mar are the Mountain Realms, inhabited by those aloof and eccentric warrior-scholars known as Rhunes, whose numbers are not accurately known. The native fauna includes a quasi-intelligent biped of placid disposition: the Fwaichi. These creatures inhabit highland forests and are protected from molestation both by statute and by local custom. For more detailed information, consult the catalogue.' "

Pardero went to the globe and presently discovered Port Mar. To the east rose a succession of enormous mountain ranges, the high crags rising past the timber line, up past snow and glaciers, into regions where rain and snowfall no longer existed. A multitude of small rivers drained the region, wandering along narrow upland valleys, expanding to become lakes, pouring over precipices to reconstitute themselves in new lakes or new streams below. Certain of the valleys were named: Haun, Gorgetto, Zangloreis, Eccord, Wintaree, Disbague, Morluke, Tuillin, Scharrode, Ronduce, a dozen others, all sounding of an odd or archaic dialect. Some of the names lay easy on his tongue, as if he well knew their proper pronunciation; and when Kolodin, peering over his shoulder, read them off, he noticed the faulty inflections, though he told Kolodin nothing of this.

Ollave called him and indicated a tall glass case. "What do you think of this?"

"Who are they?"

"An eiodarkal trismet."

"Those words mean nothing to me."

"They are Rhune terms, of course; I thought you might recognize them. An 'eiodark' is a high-ranking baron; 'trisme' is an institution analogous to marriage. 'Trismet' designates the people involved."

Pardero inspected the two figures. Both were represented to be tall, spare, dark-haired, and fair of complexion. The man wore a complicated costume of dark red cloth, a vest of black metal strips, a ceremonial helmet contrived of black metal and black fabric. The woman wore garments somewhat simpler: a long shapeless gown of gray gauze, white slippers, a loose black cap which framed the white starkly modeled features.

"Typical Rhunes," said Ollave. "They totally reject cosmopolitan standards and styles. Notice them as they stand there. Observe the cool and dispassionate expressions. Notice also, their garments have no elements in common, a clear signal that in the Rhune society male and female roles differ. Each is a mystery to the other; they might be members of different races!" He glanced sharply at Pardero. "Do they suggest anything to you?"

"They are not strange, no more than the language was strange at Carfaunge."

"Just so." Crossing the chamber to a projection screen, Ollave touched buttons. "Here is Port Mar, on the edge of the highlands."

A voice from the screen supplied a commentary to the scene. "You view the city Port Mar as you might from an aircar approaching from the south. The time is aud, which is to say, full daylight, with Furad, Maddar, Osmo, and Cirse in the sky."

The screen displayed a panorama of small residences half-concealed by foliage: structures built of dark timber and pink-tan stucco. The roofs rose at steep pitches, joining in all manner of irregular angles and eccentric gables: a style quaint and unusual. In many cases the houses had been extended and enlarged, the additions growing casually from the old structures like crystals growing from crystals. Other structures, abandoned, had fallen into ruins. "These houses were built by Majars, the original inhabitants of Marune. Very few pure-blooded Majars remain; the race is almost extinct, and Majartown is falling into disuse. The Majars, with the Rhunes, named the planet, which originally was known as 'Majar-Rhune'. The Rhunes, arriving upon Marune, decimated the Majars, but were expelled by the Whelm into the eastern mountains, where to this day they are allowed no weapons of energy or attack."

The angle of view shifted to a hostelry of stately proportions. The commentator spoke: "Here you see the Royal Rhune Hotel, invariably patronized by those Rhunes who must visit Port Mar. The management is attentive to the special and particular Rhune needs."

The view shifted across a river to a district somewhat more modern. "You now observe the New Town," said the commentator. "The Port Mar College of Arts and Technics, situated nearby, claims a distinguished faculty and almost ten thousand students, deriving both from Port Mar and from the agricultural tracts to the south and west. There are no Rhunes in attendance at the college."

Pardero asked Ollave, "And why is that?"

"The Rhunes prefer their own educational processes."

"They seem an unusual people."

"In many respects."

"So it would seem. Let us look into the Mountain Realms." Ollave consulted an index. "First I'll show you one of the autochthones: the Fwai-chi, as they are called." He touched a button, to reveal a high mountainside patched with snow and sparsely forested with gnarled black trees. The view expanded toward one of these trees, to center upon the rugose brown-black trunk, which stirred and moved. Away from the tree shambled a bulky brown-black biped with a loose pelt, all shags and tatters. The commentator spoke: "Here you see a Fwai-chi. These creatures, after their own fashion, are intelligent, and as such they are protected by the Connatic. The shags of its skin are not merely camouflage against the snow bears; they are organs for the production of hormones and the reproductive stimule. Occasionally the Fwai-chi will be seen nibbling each other; they are ingesting a stuff which reacts with a bud on the wall of their stomachs. The bud develops into an infant, which in due course is vomited into the world. Along the trailing fringes of other shags other semivital stimules are produced.

"The Fwai-chi are placid, but not helpless if provoked too far; indeed they are said to possess important parapsychic competence, and no one dares molest them."

The view shifted, down the mountainside to the valley floor. A village of fifty stone houses occupied a meadow beside the river; from a bluff a tall mansion, or castle, overlooked the valley. To Kolodin's eye, the mansion, or castle, evinced an archaic overelaboration of shape and detail; additionally the proportions appeared cramped, the construction disproportionately heavy, the windows too few, too tall and narrow. He put to Pandero a question: "What do you think of this?"

"I don't remember it." Pardero raised his hands to his temples, pressed and rubbed. "I feel pressure; I want to see no more."

"Certainly not," declared Ollave jauntily. "We'll go at once." And he added: "Come up to my office; I'll pour you a sedative, and you'll feel less perturbation."

Returning to the Connatic's Hospital, Pardero sat silently for most of the trip. At last he asked Kolodin: "How soon can I go to Marune?"

"Whenever you like," said Kolodin, and then added, in the tentative voice of a person hoping to persuade a captious child: "But why hurry? Is the hospital so dreary? Take a few weeks to study and learn, and to make some careful plans."

"I want to learn two names: my own and that of my enemy."

Kolodin blinked. He had miscalculated the intensity of Pardero's emotions. "Perhaps no enemy exists," stated Kolodin somewhat ponderously. "He is not absolutely necessary to your condition."

Pardero managed a small sour smile. "When I arrived at the Carfaunge spaceport, my hair had been hacked short. I considered it a mystery until I saw the simulated Rhune eiodark. Did you notice his hair?"

"It was combed straight over the scalp and down across the neck."

"And this is a distinctive style?"

"Well—it's hardly common, though not bizarre or

unique. It is distinctive enough to facilitate identification."

Pardero nodded gloomily. "My enemy intended that no one should identify me as a Rhune. He cut my hair, dressed me in a clown's suit, then put me on a spaceship and sent me across the Cluster, hoping I would never return."

"So it would seem. Still, why did he not simply kill you and roll you into a ditch? How much more decisive!"

"Rhunes fear killing, except in war: this I have learned from Ollave."

Kolodin surreptitiously studied Pardero who sat brooding across the landscape. Remarkable the alteration! In a few hours, from a person uninformed, vague, and confused, Pardero had become a man purposeful and integrated; a man, so Kolodin would guess, of strong passions under stern control, and after all was not this the way of the Rhunes? "For the sake of argument, let us assume that this enemy exists," said Kolodin laboriously. "He knows you; you do not know him. You will arrive at Port Mar at a disadvantage, and perhaps at considerable risk."

Pardero seemed almost amused. "So then, must I avoid Port Mar? I reckon on this risk; I intend to prepare against it."

"And how will you so prepare?"

"First I want to learn as much as possible about the Rhunes."

"Simple enough," said Kolodin. "The knowledge is in Chamber 933. What next?"

"I have not yet decided."

Sensing evasion, Kolodin pursed his lips. "The Connatic's law is exact: Rhunes are allowed neither energy weapons nor airvehicles."

Pardero grinned. "I am no Rhune until I learn my identity."

"In a technical sense, this is true," said Kolodin cautiously.

Something over a month later Kolodin accompanied Pardero to the Central Spaceport at Commarice, and out across the field to the *Dylas Extranuator*. The two said good-by at the embarcation ramp. "I probably will never see you again," said Kolodin, "and much as I would like to know the outcome of your quest, I probably will never learn."

Pardero responded in a flat voice: "I thank you for your help and for your personal kindness."

From a Rhune, thought Kolodin, even an occluded Rhune, this was almost effusiveness. He spoke in a guarded voice: "A month ago you hinted of your need for a weapon. Have you obtained such an item?"

"No," said Pardero. "I thought to wait until I was beyond the range of the Connatic's immediate attention, so to speak."

With furtive glances to left and right Kolodin tucked a small carton into Pardero's pocket. "You now carry a Dys Model G Skull-splitter. Instructions are included in the package. Don't flourish it about; the laws are explicit. Good-by, good luck, and communicate with me if possible."

"Again, thank you." Pardero clasped Kolodin's shoulders, then turned away and boarded the ship.

Kolodin returned to the terminal and ascended to the observation deck. Half an hour later he watched the black, red, and gold spaceship loft into the air, slide off and away from Numenes.

Chapter 4

★ ★ ★

During the month previous to his departure, Pardero spent many hours in Chamber 933 along the Ring of Worlds. Kolodin occasionally kept him company; Oswen Ollave, as often, came down from his offices to discuss the perplexing habits of the Rhunes.

Ollave prepared a chart which he insisted that Pardero memorize.

<table>
<tr><th></th><th>FURAD</th><th>OSMO</th><th>MADDAR</th><th>CIRSE</th></tr>
<tr><td>AUD</td><td>X</td><td>X</td><td>X
EITHER</td><td>X
OR BOTH</td></tr>
<tr><td>ISP</td><td></td><td>X</td><td>X</td><td rowspan="2">WITH OR
X
WITHOUT</td></tr>
<tr><td>CHILL ISP</td><td></td><td>X</td><td></td></tr>
<tr><td>UMBER</td><td>X</td><td></td><td>X
EITHER</td><td>X
OR BOTH</td></tr>
<tr><td>LORN UMBER</td><td>X</td><td></td><td></td><td></td></tr>
<tr><td>ROWAN</td><td></td><td></td><td>X</td><td>X</td></tr>
<tr><td>RED ROWAN</td><td></td><td></td><td>X</td><td></td></tr>
<tr><td>GREEN ROWAN</td><td></td><td></td><td></td><td>X</td></tr>
<tr><td>MIRK</td><td></td><td></td><td></td><td></td></tr>
</table>

"The chart indicates Marune's ordinary conditions of daylight,* during which the character of the landscape changes profoundly. The population is naturally affected, and most especially the Rhunes." Ollave's voice had taken on a pedantic suavity, and he enunciated his words with precision. "Port Mar is hardly notable for sophistication. The Rhunes, however, consider Port Mar a most worldly place, characterized by shameless alimentation, slackness, laxity, and a kind of bestial lasciviousness to which they apply the term 'sebalism.'

* These are the modes recognized by the folk of Port Mar. Both the Majars and the Rhunes make more elaborate distinctions.

The progression of the modes is rendered complex by reason of the diurnal rotation of Marune, the revolution of Marune around Furad, the motion of Furad and Osmo around each other, the orbital motions of Maddar and Cirse, around each other and jointly around the Furad–Osmo system. The planes of no two orbiting systems are alike.

The Fwai-chi, who lack all knowledge of astronomy, can reliably predict the modes for as far in the future as anyone cares to inquire.

Among the low mountains south of Port Mar live a 'lost' community of about ten thousand Majars, decadent, inbred, and gradually diminishing in numbers. These folks are slavishly affected by the modes of day. They regulate their moods, diet, attire, and activities by the changes. During mirk, the Majars lock themselves in their huts, and by the light of oil lamps chant imprecations against Galula the Goblin who mauls and eviscerates anyone unlucky enough to be abroad after dark. Some such entity as Galula indeed exists, but has never been satisfactorily identified.

The Rhunes, as proud and competent as the Majars are demoralized, are also strongly affected by the changing modes. Behavior proper during one mode may be considered absurd or in poor taste during another. Persons advance their erudition and hone their special skills during aud, isp, and umber. Formal ceremonies tend to take place during isp, as well as during the remarkable Ceremony of Odors. It may be noted that music is considered hyperemotional and inducive to vulgar conduct; it is never heard in the Rhune Realms. Aud is the appropriate time to go forth to battle, to conduct litigation, fight a duel, collect rent. Green rowan is a time for poetry and sentimental musing; red rowan allows the Rhune slightly to relax his etiquette. A man may condescend to take a glass of wine in company with other men, all using etiquette screens; women similarly may sip cordials or brandy. Chill isp inspires the Rhune with a thrilling ascetic exultation, which completely supersedes lesser emotions of love, hate, jealousy, greed. Conversation occurs in a hushed archaic dialect; brave ventures are planned; gallant resolves sworn; schemes of glory proposed and ratified, and many of these projects become fact, and go into the Book of Deeds.

"In the Old Town at Port Mar a handful of exiles live—young Rhunes who have rebelled against their society, or who have been ejected for lapses of conduct. They are a demoralized, miserable, and bitter group; all criticize their parents, who, so they claim, have withheld counsel and guidance. To a certain exent this is true; Rhunes feel that their precepts are self-evident even to the understanding of a child—which of course they are not; nowhere in the Cluster are conventions more arbitrary. For instance, the process of ingesting food is considered as deplorable as the final outcome of digestion, and eating is done as privately as possible. The child is supposed to arrive at this viewpoint as well as other Rhune conventions automatically. He is expected to excel in arcane and impractical skills; he must quell his sebalism."

Pardero stirred restlessly. "You have used this word before; I do not understand it."

"It is the special Rhune concept for sexuality, which the Rhunes find disgusting. How then do they procreate? It is cause for wonder. But they have solved the problem with elegance and ingenuity. During mirk, in the dark of the suns, they undergo a remarkable transformation. Do you wish to hear about it? If so, you must allow me a measure of discursiveness, as the subject is most wonderful!

"About once a month, the land grows dark, and the Rhunes become restless. Some lock themselves into their homes; others array themselves in odd costumes and go forth into the night where they perform the most astonishing deeds. The baron whose rectitude is unquestioned robs and beats one of his tenants. A staid matron commits daring acts of unmentionable depravity. No one who allows himself to be accessible is safe. What a mystery then! How to reconcile such conduct with the decorum of daylight? No one tries to do so; night-deeds are considered hardships for which no one is held responsible, like nightmares. Mirk is a time of unreality. Events during mirk are unreal, and guilt has no basis.

"During mirk, sebalism is rampant. Indeed, sexual activity occurs as a night-deed, only in the guise of rape. Marriage—'trisme,' as it is called—is never considered a sexual pairing, but rather an alliance—a joining of economic or political forces. Sexual acts, if they occur, will be night-deeds—acts of purported rape. The male participant wears a black garment over his shoulders, arms, and upper chest, and boots of black cloth. Over his head he wears a man-mask. His torso is naked. He is purposely grotesque, an abstraction of male sexuality. His costume depersonalizes him and maximizes the fantasy or unreal element. The man enters the chamber where the woman sleeps, or pretends to sleep; and in utter silence copulation occurs. Neither virginity nor its absence is significant, nor are either so much as a subject for speculation. The Rhune dialect contains no such word.

"So there you have the state of 'trisme.' Between trismetics friendships may exist, but the two address each other formally. Intimacy between any two people is rare. Rooms are large, so that folk need not huddle together, nor even approach. No person purposely touches another; in fact the occupations which require physical contact, such as barbering, doctoring, clothes-fitting, are considered pariah trades. For such services the Rhunes journey into Port Mar. A parent neither strikes nor caresses his child; a warrior attempts to kill his enemy at a distance, and weapons such as swords and daggers have only ceremonial function.

"Now allow me to describe the act of eating. On those rare occasions when a Rhune is forced to dine in the company of others he ingests his food behind a napkin, or at the back of a device unique to Marune: a screen on a metal pedestal, placed before the diner's face. At formal banquets no food is served—only wafts of varied and complicated odors, the selection and presentation being considered a creative skill.

"The Rhunes lack humor. They are highly sensitive to insult; a Rhune will never submit to ridicule. Life-long friends must reckon with each other's sensibilities and then rely upon a complicated etiquette to lubricate social occasions. In short, it seems as if the Rhunes deny themselves all the usual human pleasures. What do they substitute?

"In the first place, the Rhune is exquisitely sensitive to his landscapes of mountain, meadow, forest, and sky—all changing with the changing modes of day. He reckons his land by its aesthetic appeal; he will connive a lifetime to gain a few choice areas. He enjoys pomp, protocol, heraldic minutiae; his niceties and graces are judged as carefully as the figures of a ballet. He prides himself on his collection of sherliken scales; or the emeralds which he has mined, cut, and polished with his own hands; or his Arah magic wheels, imported from halfway across the Gaean Reach. He will perfect himself in special mathematics, or an ancient language, or the lore of fanfares, or all three, or three other abstrusities. His calligraphy and draftsmanship are taken for granted; his life work is his Book of Deeds, which he executes and illustrates and decorates with fervor and exactitude. A few of these books have reached the market; in the Reach they command enormous prices as curios.

"The Rhune is not a likeable man. He is so sensitive as to be truculent; he is contemptuous of all other races than the Rhune. He is self-centered, arrogant, unsympathetic in his judgments.

"Naturally I allude to the typical Rhune, from whom an individual may deviate, and everything I have said applies no less to the women as the men.

"The Rhunes display correspondingly large virtues:

dignity, courage, honor, intellects of incomprehensible complexity—though here again individuals may differ from the norm.

"Anyone who owns land considers himself an aristocrat, and the hierarchy descends from kaiark, through kang, eiodark, baronet, baron, knight, and squire. The Fwai-chi have retreated from the Realms, but still make their pilgrimages through the upper forests and along the high places. There is no interaction between the two races.

"Needless to say, among a people so passionate, proud, and reckless, and so anxious to expand their land holdings, conflict is not unknown. The force of the Connatic's Second Edict and, more effectively, an embargo upon energy weapons, has eliminated formal war. But raids and forays are common, and enmities last forever. The rules of warfare are based upon two principles. First, no man may attack a person of higher rank than himself; second, since blood violence is a mirk-deed, killing is achieved at a distance with blast-bolts; aristocrats however use swords and so demonstrate fortitude. Ordinary warriors will not look at a man in the face and kill him; such an act haunts a man forever—unless the act is done by mirk, when it becomes no more than a nightmare. But only if unplanned. Premeditated murder by mirk is vile murder."

Pardero said, "Now I know why my enemy sent me off to Bruse-Tansel instead of leaving me dead in a ditch."

"There is a second argument against murder: it cannot be concealed. The Fwai-chi detect crimes, and no one escapes; it is said that they can taste a dead man's blood and cite all the circumstances of his death."

On this evening Pardero and Kolodin chose to spend the night in the tourist chambers on the lower decks of the tower. Kolodin made a videophone call and returned with a slip of paper, which he handed to Pardero. "The results of my inquiries. I asked myself, what ship leaving Port Mar would land you at Carfaunge Spaceport on tenth Mariel Gaean? Traffic Central's computer provided a name and a date. On 2 Ferario Gaean the *Berenicia* of the Black and Red Line departed Port Mar. More than likely you were aboard."

Pardero tucked the paper into his pocket. "Another matter which concerns me: how do I pay my passage to Marune? I have no money."

Kolodin made an expansive gesture. "No difficulties there. Your rehabilitation includes an extra thousand ozols for just this purpose. Any more worries?"

Pardero grinned. "Lots of them."

"You'll have an interesting time of it," said Kolodin.

The *Dylas Extranuator* drove out past the Pentagram, circled the diadem in the horn of the Unicorn, and coasted into Tsambara, Alastor 1317. Here Pardero made connection with a ship of the Black and Red Line which, after touching into a number of remote little places, veered off along the Fontinella Wisp and presently approached an isolated system of four dwarfs respectively orange, blue, green, and red.

Marune, Alastor 933, expanded below, to show a surface somewhat dark and heavy-textured below its fleets and shoals of clouds. The ship descended and settled upon the Port Mar Spaceport. Pardero and a dozen other passengers alighted, surrendered their last ticket coupon, passed through the lobby and out upon the soil of Marune.

The time was isp. Osmo glared blue halfway up the southern sky; Maddar rode at the zenith; Cirse peered over the northeast horizon. The light was a trifle cold, but rich with those overtones provided by Maddar and Cirse, so that objects cast a three-phase shadow.

Pardero halted before the terminal, looked around the landscape, across the sky, inhaled a deep breath, exhaled. The air tasted fresh, cool, and tart, unlike both the dank air of Bruse-Tansel and the warm sweet air of Numenes. The suns sliding in different directions across the sky, the subtle lights, the taste of the air, soothed an ache in his mind he had not heretofore noticed. A mile to the west the structures of Port Mar stood clear and crisp: beyond the land fell away. The view seemed not at all strange. Whence came the familiarity? From research in Chamber 933? Or from his own experience? To the east the land swelled and rose in receding masses of ever higher mountains, reaching up to awesome heights. The peaks gleamed white with snow and gray with granite scree; below, bands of dark forest muffled the slopes. Mass collided with light to create shape and shadow; the clarity of the air as it swept through the spaces was almost palpable.

The waiting bus sounded an impatient chime; Pardero slowly climbed aboard, and the bus moved off along the Avenue of Strangers toward Port Mar.

The attendant made an announcement: "First stop, the Traveler's Inn. Second, the Outworld Inn. Then the Royal Rhune Hotel. Then over the bridge into New Town for the Cassander Inn and the University Inn."

Pardero chose the Outworld Inn which seemed sufficiently large and impersonal. Imminence hung in the air, so heavy that his enemy must also be oppressed.

Pardero cautiously surveyed the lobby of the Outworld Inn, but saw only off-world folk who paid him no heed. The hotel personnel ignored him. So far, so good.

He took a lunch of soup, cold meat, and bread in the dining room, as much to compose himself as to appease his appetite. He lingered at the table reviewing his plans. To broadcast the fewest ripples of disturbance, he must move softly, delicately, working from the periphery inward.

He left the hotel and sauntered back up the Avenue of Strangers toward the green-glass dome of the spaceport terminal. As he walked, Osmo dipped low and sank behind the western edge of Port Mar. Isp became rowan, with Cirse and Maddar yet in the sky, to produce a warm soft light that hung in the air like haze.

Arriving at the terminal, Pardero entered and went to the reception desk. The clerk came forward—a small portly man with the cinnamon skin and golden eyes of an upper-caste Majar, one of those who lived in the timber and stucco houses on the slopes at the back of Old Town.

"How may I serve you, sir?"

Clearly Pardero aroused in his mind no quiver of recognition.

"Perhaps you can provide me some information," said Pardero. "On or about 2 Ferario, I took passage aboard the *Berenicia* of the Black and Red Line. One of the other passengers asked me to perform a small errand, which I was unable to achieve. Now I must notify him but I have forgotten his name, and I would like to glance at the relevant passenger list."

"No difficulties here, sir; the ledger is easily consulted." A display screen lit up; the clerk turned a knob; figures and listings flicked past. "Here we are at 2 Ferario. Quite correct, sir. The *Berenicia* arrived, took aboard eight passengers, and departed."

Pardero studied the passenger list. "Why are the names in different columns?"

"By order of the Demographical Institute, so that they may gauge traffic between the worlds. Here are transients upon Marune taking departure. These names—only two, as you see—represent folk of Marune bound for other worlds."

"My man would be one of these. Which ones took passage to Bruse-Tansel?"

The clerk, somewhat puzzled, consulted the list. "Neither. Baron Shimrod's destination was Xampias. The Noble Serle Glaize boarded the ship on an 'open' ticket."

"What sort of ticket is this?"

"It is often purchased by a tourist who lacks a fixed destination. The ticket provides a stipulated number of travel-units; when these are exhausted the tourist purchases further units to fit his particular needs."

"This 'open ticket' used by Serle Glaize, how far might it have taken him? To Bruse-Tansel, for instance?"

"The *Berenicia* does not put into Bruse-Tansel, but let me see. One hundred and forty-eight ozols to Dadarnisse Junction; to Bruse-Tansel one hundred and two ozols . . . Yes, indeed. You will notice that the Noble Serle Glaize bought an open ticket to the value of two hundred and fifty ozols; to Bruse-Tansel exactly."

"So: Serle Glaize. This is my man." Pardero reflected upon the name. It lacked all resonance, all familiar flavor. He passed two ozols across the counter to the clerk, who took them with grave courtesy.

Pardero asked: "Who sold the ticket to Serle Glaize?"

"The initial is 'Y'; that would be Yanek, on the next shift."

"Perhaps you could telephone Yanek and ask if he recalls the circumstances. I will pay five ozols for significant information."

The clerk eyed Pardero sidelong. "What sort of information do you consider significant?"

"Who bought the ticket? I doubt if Serle Glaize did so himself. He must have come with a companion whose identity I wish to learn."

The clerk went to a telephone and spoke in a

guarded manner, from time to time glancing over his shoulder toward Pardero. At last he returned, his manner somewhat subdued. "Yanek barely recalls the matter. He believes that the ticket was bought by a person in a black Rhune cape, who also wore a gray casque with a visor and malar flaps, so that his features made no impression upon Yanek. The time was busy; Yanek was preoccupied and noticed no more."

"This is not the information I require," Pardero grumbled. "Is there anyone who can tell me more?"

"I can think of no one, sir."

"Very well." Pardero counted down another two ozols. "This is for your kind cooperation."

"Thank you, sir. Allow me to make a suggestion. The Rhunes who visit Port Mar without exception use the Royal Rhune Hotel. Information, however, may be hard to come by."

"Thank you for the suggestion."

"Are you not a Rhune yourself, sir?"

"After a fashion, yes."

The clerk nodded and uttered a soft chuckle. "A Majar will mistake a Rhune never indeed, oh never . . ."

In a pensive mood Pardero returned along the Avenue of Strangers. The learned computations of M.T. Rady, the sociopsychic deductions of Oswen Ollave had been validated. Still, by what obscure means had the Majar recognized him? His features were not at all peculiar; his pigmentation was hardly distinctive; his clothes and hairstyle were, by cosmopolitan standards, ordinary enough; in short, he differed little from any other guest at the Outworld Inn. No doubt he betrayed himself by unconscious gestures or attitudes; perhaps he was more of a Rhune than he felt himself to be.

The Avenue of Strangers ended at the river; as Pardero reached the bridge Maddar slanted behind the western lowlands; Cirse moved slowly up the sky:

green rowan. Green ripples flickered across the water; the white walls of New Town shone pale apple-green. Along the riverfront festoons of lights appeared, indicating places of entertainment: beer gardens, dance pavilions, restaurants. Pardero scowled at the brashness of the scene, then gave a soft rueful snort. Had he surprised a set of Rhune attitudes surfacing through his amnesia?

Pardero turned into the narrow Street of Brass Boxes, which curved gradually up-slope, between ancient structures of age-blackened wood. The shops facing out upon the street uniformly showed a pair of high windows, a brass-bound door, and only the most unobtrusive indication as to their wares, as if each strove to exceed his neighbor in reserve.

The Street of Brass Boxes ended in a dim shadowed square, surrounded by curio shops, bookstores, specialty houses of many varieties. Pardero saw his first Rhunes, moving from shop to shop, pondering the merchandise, indicating their needs to the Majar shopkeepers with indifferent flicks of the finger. None of them so much as glanced toward Pardero, which caused him irrationally mixed feelings.

He crossed the square and turned up the Avenue of Black Jangkars to an arched portal in a stone wall. He passed beneath and approached the Royal Rhune Hotel. He halted before the vestibule. Once inside the Royal Rhune there could be no turning back; he must accept the consequences of his return to Marune.

Through the tall doors stepped two men and a woman—the men wearing costumes of beige and black with dark red sashes, so similar as to suggest military uniforms; the woman, almost as tall as either of the men, wore a tight blue-gray suit, with an indigo cape draping from black epaulettes: a mode considered suitable for visits to Port Mar, where the formal gauze gowns of the Realms were inappropriate. The three marched past Pardero, each allowing him a single glance. Pardero sensed no flicker of recognition. Small cause for surprise since the Rhunes numbered well over a hundred thousand.

Pardero pushed aside the tall gaunt doors which seemed a part of the Rhune architectural environment. The lobby was an enormous high-ceilinged room with sounds echoing across a bare russet and black tile floor. The chairs were upholstered in leather. The central table displayed a variety of technical magazines and at the far end of the room a rack held brochures advertising tools, chemicals, craft supplies, papers and inks, rare woods and stone. A tall narrow arch flanked by columns of fluted green stone communicated with the office. Pardero looked briefly around the lobby and passed through the arch.

A clerk of advanced age rose to his feet and approached the counter; despite age, a bald head, and unctuous wattles, his manner was alert and punctilious. In an instant he assessed Pardero, his garments and mannerisms, and performed a bow of precisely calibrated courtesy. "How can we oblige you, sir?" As he spoke a trace of uncertainty seemed to enter his manner.

"Several months ago," said Pardero, "about the first of Ferario to be more precise, I was a guest at this hotel, and I wish to refresh my recollections. Will you be so good as to show me the records for this date?"

"As you require, Your Dignity."* The clerk turned Pardero a second half-surreptitious side-glance, and his manner altered even further, becoming tinged with doubt, or uneasiness, or even anxiety. He bent with an almost audible creaking of vertebrae and elevated a leather-bound ledger to the counter. With a reverential

* The all-purpose honorific, somewhat more respectful than a simple 'sir,' to be applied to Rhunes of indeterminate status.

flourish he parted the covers, and one by one turned the pages, each of which displayed a schematic chart of the hotel's accommodations, with notations in inks of various colors. "Here, Dignity, is the date you mention. If you choose to advise me, I will assist you."

Pardero inspected the ledger, but could not decipher the archaic calligraphy.

In a voice meant to convey an exquisite and comprehensive discretion the clerk spoke on. "On this phase our facilities were not overextended. In our 'Sincere Courtesy' wing, we housed the trismets* of various gentlefolk. You will notice the chambers so indicated. In our 'Approbation' accommodations we served the Eiodark Torde and the Wirwove Ippolita, with their respective trismets. The 'Altitude' suite was occupied by the Kairak Rianlle of Eccord, the Kraiak Dervas, the Lissolet Maerio. In the 'Hyperion' suite we entertained the late Kaiark Jochaim of Scharrode, may his ghost be quickly appeased, with the Kraike Singhalissa, the Kangs Efraim and Destian, and the Lissolet Sthelany." The clerk turned his trembling and dubious smile upon Pardero. "Do I not now have the honor of addressing His Force the new Kaiark of Scharrode?"

Pardero said somewhat ponderously: "You recognize me then?"

"Yes, Your Force, now that I have spoken with you. I admit to confusion; your presence has altered in a way which I hardly know how to explain. You seem, shall we say, more mature, more controlled, and of course your foreign garments enhance these differences.

* Trismet: The group of persons resulting from a 'trisme,' the Rhune analog of marriage. These persons might be a man and his trismetic female partner; or a man, the female partner, one or more of her children (of which the man may or may not be the sire). 'Family' approximates the meaning of 'trismet' but carries a package of inaccurate and inapplicable connotations. Paternity is often an uncertain determination; rank and status, therefore, are derived from the mother.

But I am certain that I am right." The clerk peered in sudden doubt. "Am I not, Your Force?"

Pardero smiled coolly. "How could you demonstrate the fact one way or the other without my assurance?"

The clerk muffled an exclamation. Muttering under his breath he brought to the counter a second leather-bound volume, twice the size of the ledger. He glanced peevishly toward Pardero, then turned thick pages of pale brown parchment.

Pardero asked: "What book is that?"

The clerk looked up from the pages, and now his gray old lips sagged incredulously. "I have here the Great Rhune Almanac. Are you not familiar with it?"

Pardero managed a curt nod. "Show me the folk who occupied the Hyperion suite."

"Inexorable Force, I was about to do so." The clerk turned pages. On the left were genealogical charts, ladders, linkages, and trees, indited in rich inks of various colors; on the right photographs were arranged in patterns relative to the charts: thousands upon thousands of names, an equal number of likenesses. The clerk turned pages with maddening deliberation. At last he halted, pondered a moment, then tapped the page with his finger. "The lineage of Scharrode."

Pardero could restrain himself no longer. He turned the volume about and studied the photographs.

Halfway down the page a pale-haired man of middle maturity looked forth. His face, angular and bleak, suggested an interesting complexity of character. The forehead might have been that of a scholar, the wide mouth seemed composed against some unwelcome or unfashionable emotion, such as humor. The superscription read: *Jochaim, House of Benbuphar, Seventy-ninth Kaiark.*

A green linkage led to the still face of a woman, her expression unfathomable. The caption read: *Alferica, House of Jent.* Below, a heavy maroon line led to the countenance of an unsmiling young man: a face which Pardero recognized as his own. The caption read: *Efraim, House of Benbuphar, Kang of the Realm.*

At least I now know my name, thought Pardero. I am Efraim, and I was Kang, and now I am Kaiark. I am a man of high rank! He looked up at the clerk, surprising a shrewd and intent scrutiny. "You are curious," said Efraim. "There is no mystery. I have been off-planet and have just returned. I know nothing of what has happened in my absence. The Kaiark Jochaim is dead?"

"Yes, Your Force. There has been uncertainty and confusion, so I understand. You have been the subject of concern, since now, of course, you are the Eightieth Kaiark, and the allowable lapse has almost transpired."

Efraim nodded slowly. "So now I am Kaiark of Scharrode." He returned to the almanac, conscious of the clerk's gaze.

The other faces on the page were three. From Jochaim a second green line descended to the face of a handsome dark-haired woman with a pale high forehead, blazing black eyes, a keen high-bridged nose. The caption identified her as *Kraike Singhalissa.* From Singhalissa vermilion lines led first to a dark-haired young man with the aquiline features of his mother: Kang Destian, and a girl, dark-haired and pale, with pensive features and a mouth drooping at the corners, a girl in fact of rather remarkable beauty. The caption identified her as the *Lissolet Sthelany.*

Efraim spoke in a voice he tried to keep matter-of-fact: "What do you recall of our visit here to Port Mar?"

The clerk reflected. "The two trismets, of Scharrode and Eccord, arrived in concert, and in general conducted themselves as a single party. The younger persons visited New Town, while their elders transacted business. Certain tensions became evident. There followed a discussion of the visit to New Town, of which several of the older persons disapproved. Most exercised were the Kraike Singhalissa and the Kaiark Rianlle, who thought that the expedition lacked dignity. When you failed to appear by isp 25 of the Third Cycle, everyone felt concern; evidently you had failed to apprise anyone of your departure."

"Evidently," said Efraim. "Did mirk occur during our visit?"

"No; there was no mirk."

"You heard no remarks, you recall no circumstances which might explain my departure?"

The clerk looked puzzled. "A most curious question, Your Force! I remember nothing of consequence, though I was surprised to hear that you had acquainted yourself with that off-world vagabond." He sniffed. "No doubt he took advantage of your condescension; he is known as a persuasive rogue."

"Which off-world vagabond is this?"

"What? Do you not remember exploring New Town with the fellow Lorcas?"

"I had forgotten his name. Lorcas, you say?"

"Matho Lorcas. He consorts with New Town trash; he is fugleman for all these sebal cretins at the university."

"And when did Kaiark Jochaim die?"

"Soon after his return to Scharrode, in battle against Gosso, Kaiark of Gorgetto. You have returned opportunely. In another several days you would no longer be kaiark, and I have heard that Kaiark Rianlle has proposed a trisme to unite the realms of Eccord and Scharrode. Now that you are returned, conditions may be altered." The clerk turned pages in the almanac. "Kaiark Rianlle is an intense and determined man." The clerk tapped a photograph. Efraim saw a handsome distinguished face, framed by a casque of shining silver ringlets. The Kraike Dervas looked forth blankly;

her face seemed to lack distinctive character. The same was true of the Lissolet Maerio, who stared forth expressionlessly, but who nonetheless displayed a youthful if rather vacuous prettiness.

The clerk asked cautiously: "Do you plan to stay with us, Force?"

"I think not. And I wish you to say nothing whatever of my return to Marune. I must clarify certain circumstances."

"I quite understand, Force. Thank you very much indeed!"—this last for the ten ozols which Efraim had placed on the counter.

Efraim emerged from the hotel into a melancholy umber. He walked slowly back down the Avenue of Black Jangkars, and coming once more to the square he now took time to walk around, and with awe and wonder investigated the shops. Could there exist anywhere in all Alastor Cluster a richer concentration of the arcane, the esoteric, the special? And Efraim wondered what had been his own fields of erudition, his own unique virtuosities. Whatever they were, he retained none of them; his mind was a blank.

Somewhat mournfully he proceeded down the Street of Brass Boxes to the river. New Town appeared quiet. Festoons of lights still glowed along the riverfront, but the beer gardens and cafés lacked animation. Efraim turned away, walked up the Avenue of Strangers to the Outworld Inn. He went to his chamber and slept.

He dreamt a series of vivid dreams and awoke in a flush of excitement. After a moment he tried to reform the shattered images into focus so that he might grasp the meanings which had marched across his sleeping mind. To no avail. Composing himself, he slept once more until a gong announced the hour of breakfast.

Chapter 5

★ ★ ★

Efraim emerged from the hotel into that phase sometimes known as half-aud. Furad and Osmo ruled the sky, to produce a warm yellow light, which connoisseurs of such matters considered fresh, effervescent, and gay, but lacking the richness and suavity of full aud. He stood for a moment breathing the cool air. His melancholy had diminished; better to be Kaiark Efraim of Scharrode than Efraim the butcher, or Efraim the cook, or Efraim the garbage collector.

He set along the Avenue of Strangers. Arriving at the bridge, instead of veering left into the Street of Brass Boxes he crossed into New Town, and discovered an environment totally different from that of Old Town.

The geography of New Town, so Efraim would discover, was simple. Four thoroughfares paralleled the river: the Estrada, which terminated at the university; the Avenue of the Agency; then the Avenue of Haune and the Avenue of Douaune, after Osmo's two small dead planets.

Efraim walked westward along the Estrada, examining the cafés and beer gardens with wistful interest. To his present perspective they seemed almost flagrantly innocent. He stepped into one of the beer gardens and glanced toward the young man and girl who sat huddled so closely together. Could he ever feel so easily licentious in full view of everyone? Perhaps even now he had not escaped the strictures of his past, which after all was less than six months gone.

He approached a portly man in a white apron who seemed to be the manager. "Sir, are you acquainted with a certain Matho Lorcas?"

"Matho Lorcas? I do not know the gentleman."

Efraim continued west along the Estrada and presently at a booth devoted to the sale of off-world periodicals the name 'Matho Lorcas' sparked recognition. The girl attendant pointed along the avenue: "Ask there, in the Satyr's Cave. You might find him at work. If not, they know his dwelling."

Mathos Lorcas was indeed at work, serving mugs of beer along the bar. He was a tall young man with a keen vivacious face. His dark hair was cut short in a casual and unassuming style. When he spoke his thin crooked mouth worked dozens of changes across his face. Efraim watched him a moment before approaching. Matho Lorcas was a person whose humor, intelligence, and easy flamboyance might well excite the antagonism of less favored individuals. Hard to suspect malice, or even guile, in Matho Lorcas. The fact remained that soon after making Lorcas' acquaintance Efraim had been rendered mindless and shipped off across the Cluster.

Efraim approached the bar and took a seat; Lorcas approached. Efraim asked. "You are Matho Lorcas?"

"Yes indeed!"

"Do you recognize me?"

Lorcas gave Efraim a frowning scrutiny. His face cleared. "You are the Rhune! I forget your name."

"Efraim, of Scharrode."

"I remember you well, and the two girls you escorted. How grave and proper their behavior! You have changed! In fact you seem a different person. How goes life in your mountain realm?"

"As usual, or so I suppose. I am most anxious to have a few words with you. When will you be free?"

"At any time. Right now, if you like; I am bored with the work. Ramono! Take charge of affairs!" He ducked under the bar and asked of Efraim: "Will you take a mug of beer? Or perhaps a glass of Del wine?"

"No thank you." Efraim had decided upon a policy of caution and reserve. "It is early in the day for me."

"Just as you like. Come, let us sit over here where we can watch the river flow by. So. Do you know, I have often wondered about you, and how you eventually—well, shall we say, accommodated yourself to your dilemma, pleasant though it might have been."

"How do you mean?"

"The two beautiful girls you escorted—though I realize in the Mountain Realms things aren't done quite so easily."

Aware that he must seem dense and dull, Efraim asked: "What do you recall of the occasion?"

Lorcas held up his hands in protest. "So long ago? After so many other occasions? Let me think . . ." He grinned. "I deceive you. In truth, I've thought long and often of those two girls, so alike, so different, and oh, how wasted in those ineffable Mountain Realms! They walk and talk like enchanted blocks of ice—though I suspect that one or the other, or both, under the proper circumstances might easily melt; and I for one would rejoice to arrange such circumstances. You consider me sebal? I'm far worse; I'm positively chorastic!"* He glanced sidelong toward Efraim. "You don't seem appalled, or even shocked. For a fact you *are* a person different from the earnest young Kang of six months ago."

"This may well be true," said Efraim without impatience. "Returning to that occasion, what happened?"

* Chorasm: Sebalism carried to a remarkable extreme.

Lorcas turned Efraim another quizzical side-glance. "You don't remember?"

"Not well."

"Odd. You seemed quite alert. You recall how we met?"

"Not too well."

Lorcas gave a half-incredulous shrug. "I had just stepped out of the Caduceus Book Shop. You approached and asked directions to the Fairy Gardens, where at the time Galligade's Puppets were entertaining. The mode as I recall was low aud, going into umber, which always seems to me to be a rather festive time. I noted that you and the Kang Destian—so I recall his name—escorted not one but two pretty girls, and I'd never had the opportunity to meet a Rhune before, so I volunteered to conduct you in person. At the Fairy Gardens we found that Galligade had just finished his show and the disappointment of the girls prompted me to a spasm of insane altruism. I insisted on acting as your host—not my usual conduct, I assure you. I ordered a bottle of wine and etiquette screens for those who considered them necessary, and so there we were: the Lissolet Sthelany, observing me with aristocratic detachment, the other girl—I forget the name—"

"The Lissolet Maerio."

"Correct. She was only a trifle more cordial, though, mind you, I'm making no complaints. Then there was the Kang Destian, who was sardonic and surly, and yourself, who behaved with elegant formality. You were the first Rhunes I'd met, and when I found you to be of royal blood, I thought my efforts and ozols well spent.

"So we sat and drank the wine and listened to the music. More accurately, I drank wine. You and the Lissolet Maerio, thoroughly daring, sipped behind your etiquette screens. The other two declared themselves uninterested. The girls watched the students and marveled at the crassness and sebalism. I fell in love with the Lissolet Sthelany, who of course was oblivious. I used all my charm; she studied me with fascinated revulsion and presently she and Destian returned to the hotel.

"You and the Lissolet Maerio remained until Destian came back with orders that Maerio return to the hotel. You and I were left alone. I was due at the Three Lanterns; you walked up Jibberee Hill with me. I went to work; and you returned to the hotel: that's all there is to it."

Efraim heaved a deep sigh. "You did not accompany me to the hotel?"

"No. You went off by yourself, in a most unsettled mood. If I may make bold to ask—why are you so concerned about this evening?"

Efraim saw no reason to hold back the truth. "On that evening I lost my memory. I remember arriving at Carfaunge, on Bruse-Tansel, and I finally made my way to Numenes and the Connatic's Hospital. The experts declared me a Rhune. I returned to Port Mar; I arrived yesterday. At the Royal Rhune Hotel I learned my name, and I find that I am now the Kaiark of Scharrode. Other than this I know nothing. I recognize no one and nothing; my past is a blank. How can I conduct my own affairs responsibly, much less those of the Realm? I must set things right. Where do I start? How do I proceed? Why was my memory taken from me? Who took me to the spaceport and put me aboard the spaceship? How shall I explain myself to my people? If the past is empty, the future seems full, of concern and doubt and confusion. And I suspect that I will find little sympathy at home."

Lorcas gave a soft ejaculation, and sat back, his eyes glistening. "Do you know, I envy you. How lucky you are, with the mystery of your own past to solve!"

"I lack all such enthusiasm," said Efraim. "The past looms over me; I feel stifled. My enemies know me; I can only grope for them. I go out to Scharrode blind and helpless."

"The situation is not without compensations," murmured Lorcas. "Most people would gladly rule a Mountain Realm, or any realm whatever. Not a few would be pleased to inhabit the same castle with the Lissolet Sthelany."

"These compensations are all very well, but they do not expose my enemy."

"Assuming that the enemy exists."

"He exists. He put me aboard the *Berenicia* and paid my fare to Bruse-Tansel."

"Bruse-Tansel is not close. Your enemy would seem not to lack funds."

Efraim grunted. "Who knows how much money of my own I carried? Perhaps I paid my own fare out to the limit of my pocketbook."

"This would be a fine sardonic touch," Lorcas agreed. "If true, your enemy has style."

"Another possibility exists," mused Efraim. "I may be looking at the matter backwards."

"An interesting thought. In what exact regard?"

"Perhaps I committed some horrid deed which I could not bear to contemplate, thus inducing amnesia, and some person—my friend rather than my enemy—sent me away from Marune so that I might escape the penalty for my acts."

Lorcas uttered an incredulous laugh. "Your conduct in my presence was quite genteel."

"So how then, immediately after parting from you, did I lose my memory?"

Lorcas considered a moment. "This might not be so mysterious after all."

"The savants on Numenes were baffled. But you have gained an insight into my problems?"

Lorcas grinned. "I know someone who isn't a savant." He jumped to his feet. "Come along, let's visit this man."

Efraim dubiously arose. "Is it safe? You might be the guilty person. I don't want to end up on Bruse-Tansel a second time."

Lorcas chuckled. "You are a Rhune no longer. The Rhunes lack all humor; their lives are so strange that the absurd seems merely another phase of normality. I am not your secret enemy, I assure you. In the first place I lack the two or three hundred ozols to send you to Bruse-Tansel."

Efraim followed Lorcas out upon the avenue. Lorcas said: "We are bound for a rather peculiar establishment. The proprietor is an eccentric. Unkind folk consider him disreputable. At the moment he is out of vogue, owing to the efforts of the Benkenists, who are currently all the rage around the college. They affect a stoic imperturbability to everything except their inner norms, and Skogel's numbered mixtures seriously interfere with normality. As for me, I reject all fads except those of my own devising. Can you imagine what now preoccupies me?"

"No."

"The Mountain Realms. The genealogies, the waxing and waning of fortunes, the poetry and declamations, the ceremonial fumes, the gallantries and romantic postures, the eruditions, and scholarship. Do you realize that Rhune monographs circulate throughout the Cluster and the Gaean Reach as well? Do you realize that sport is unknown among the Realms? There are neither games nor frivolous recreations, not even among the children?"

"The thought never occurred to me. Where are we going?"

"Yonder, up the Street of the Clever Flea . . . Naturally you would not know how the street got its name." As they walked, Lorcas recounted the ribald legend. Efraim listened with only half an ear. They turned the corner into a street of marginal enterprises: a booth selling fried clams, a gambling arcade, a cabaret decorated with red and green lights, a bordello, a novelty shop, a travel agency, a store which displayed in the show window a stylized Tree of Life, the golden fruit labeled in a flowing unreadable script. Here Lorcas paused. "Let me do the talking, unless Skogel asks you a direct question. He has a queer manner which antagonizes everyone, but which I happen to know is spurious. Or at least I strongly suspect as much. In any event, be surprised at nothing; also, if he quotes a price, agree, no matter what your reservations. Nothing puts him off like haggling. Come along then; let's try our luck." He entered the shop with Efraim following slowly behind.

From the dimness at the back of the shop Skogel appeared: a man of medium stature, thin as a post with long arms and a round waxen face, above which rose spikes of dust-brown hair. "Pleasant modes," said Lorcas. "Have you collected yet from our friend Boodles?"

"Nothing. But I expected nothing and dealt with him accordingly."

"How so?"

"You know his requirements. He received only tincture of cacodyl in water, which may or may not have served his purposes."

"He made no complaints to me, though in truth he has seemed somewhat subdued of late."

"If he chooses, he may come to me for consolation. And who is this gentleman? Something about him seems Rhune, something else says out-world."

"You are right in both directions. He is a Rhune who has spent an appreciable time on Numenes, and Bruse-Tansel as well. You instantly wonder why. The answer is simple—he has lost his memory. I told him that if anyone could help him it would be you."

"Bah. I don't stock memories in boxes, neatly labeled like so many cathartics. He'll have to contrive his own memories. Isn't this easy enough?"

Lorcas looked at Efraim with an expression of rueful amusement. "Contrary fellow that he is, he wants his own memories back."

"He won't find them here. Where did he lose them? That's the place to look."

"An enemy stole his memory and put him on a ship to Bruse-Tansel. My friend is anxious to punish this thief, hence his set chin and gleaming eyes."

Skogel, throwing back his head, laughed and slapped the counter. "That's more like it! Too many wrongdoers escape with whole skins and profit! Revenge! There's the word! I wish you luck! Good modes, sir." And Skogel, turning his back, stalked stiff-legged back into the dimness of his shop. Efraim stared after him in wonder, but Lorcas signaled him to patience. Presently Skogel stalked forward. "And what do you require on this occasion?"

Lorcas said: "Do you recall your remarks of a week ago?"

"In regard to what?"

"Psychomorphosis."

"A large word," grumbled Skogel. "I spoke it at random."

"Would any of this apply to my friend?"

"Certainly. Why not?"

"And the source of this psychomorphosis?"

Skogel put his hands on the counter and leaning forward scrutinized Efraim with owlish intensity. "You are a Rhune?"

"Yes."

"What is your name?"

"I seem to be Efraim, Kaiark of Scharrode."

"Then you must be wealthy."

"I don't know whether I am or not."

"And you want the return of your memory?"

"Naturally."

"You have come to the wrong place. I deal in commodities of other sorts." Skogel slapped the counter and made as if to turn away again.

Lorcas said smoothly: "My friend insists that you at least accept a fee, or honorarium, for your advice."

"Fee? For words? For guesses and hypotheses? Do you take me for a man without shame?"

"Of course not!" declared Lorcas. "He only wants to learn where his memory went."

"Then this is my guess, and he may have it free of cost. He has eaten Fwai-chi shag." Skogel indicated the shelves, cases, and cabinets of his shop, which were stocked with bottles of every size and shape, crystallized herbs, stoneware jugs, metal oddments, tins, phials, jars, and an unclassifiable miscellaneity of confusing scope. "I will reveal a truth," declared Skogel portentously. "Much of my merchandise, on a functional level, is totally ineffective. Psychically, symbolically, subliminally, the story is different! Each item exerts its own sullen strength, and sometimes I feel myself in the presence of elementals. With an infusion of spider grass, mixed perhaps with pulverized devil's eye, I achieve astounding results. The Benkenists, idiots and witlings as they are, aver that only the credulous are affected; they are wrong! Our organisms swim in a paracosmic fluid, which no one can comprehend; none of our senses find scope or purchase, so to speak. Only by operative procedures, which the Benkenists deride, can we manipulate this ineffable medium; and by so stating, am I therefore a charlatan?" Skogel slapped the counter with a split-faced grin of triumph.

With delicate emphasis Lorcas inquired: "And what of the Fwai-chi?"

"Patience!" snapped Skogel. "Allow me my brief moment of vanity. After all, I do not veer too far astray."

"By all means," said Lorcas hastily. "Declaim to your heart's content."

Not altogether mollified, Skogel took up the thread of his remarks. "I have long speculated that the Fwai-chi interact with the paracosmos somewhat more readily than men, although they are a taciturn race and never explain their feats, or perhaps they take their multiplex environment for granted. In any event, they are a most peculiar and versatile race, which the Majar, at least, appreciate. I refer of course to that final poor fragment of the race who live over the hill." Skogel looked truculently from Lorcas to Efraim, but neither challenged his opinion.

Skogel continued. "A certain shaman of the Majars fancies to consider himself in my debt, and not too long ago he invited me to Atabus to witness an execution. My friend explained an innovation in Majar justice: the suspect, or the adjudged—among the Majars the distinction is slight—is dosed with Fwai-chi shag, and his reactions, which range from torpor through hallucination, antics, convulsions, frantic feats of agility, to instant death, are noted. The Majar are nothing but a pragmatic folk; they take a lively interest in the capabilities of the human organism, and consider themselves great scientists. In my presence they administered a golden-brown gum from dorsal Fwai-chi shags, and the suspect at once fancied himself four different persons who conducted a vivacious conversation among themselves and the onlookers, employing a single tongue and larynx to produce two and sometimes three voices simultaneously. My host described some of the other effects he had witnessed, and mentioned a certain shag whose exudation blotted away human memory. I therefore suggest that your friend has been dosed with

Fwai-chi shag." He peered from one to the other, showing a small trembling smile of triumph. "And that, in short, is my opinion."

"All very well," said Lorcas, "but how is my friend to be cured?"

Skogel made a careless gesture. "No cure is known, for the reason that none exists. What is gone, is gone."

Lorcas looked ruefully at Efraim. "So there you have it. Someone dosed you with Fwai-chi shag."

"I wonder who," said Efraim. "I wonder who."

Lorcas turned to speak to Skogel, but the shopkeeper had disappeared into the dim chamber at the rear of his establishment.

Lorcas and Efraim returned along the Street of the Clever Flea to the Estrada, Efraim pensive and grim. Lorcas, after darting half a dozen glances toward his companion, could no longer contain his curiosity. "So now what will you do?"

"What must be done."

Ten paces later Lorcas said: "You evidently have no fear of death."

Efraim shrugged.

Lorcas asked: "How will you achieve this business?"

"I must return to Scharrode," said Efraim. "Is there any other way? My enemy is someone I know well; would I drink with a stranger? In Port Mar were the following persons: Kaiark Jochaim, who is dead, the Kraike Singhalissa, the Kang Destian, the Lissolet Sthelany. Then, from Eccord, the Kaiark Rianlle, the Kraike Dervas, and the Lissolet Maerio. And, conceivably, Matho Lorcas, except in this case, why would you take me to Skogel?"

"Precisely so," said Lorcas. "On that distant occasion I dosed you only with good wine from which you took no harm."

"And you saw nothing significant, nothing suspicious, nothing dire?"

Lorcas reflected. "I noticed nothing overt. I felt stifled passion and flows of emotion, but where they led I could not divine. To be candid, I expected strange personalities among the Rhunes, and I made no attempt to understand what I saw. Without a memory you will also be handicapped."

"Very likely. But now I am Kaiark and everyone must go at my pace. I can recover my memory at leisure. What is the best transportation to Scharrode?"

"There's no choice," said Lorcas. "You hire an aircar and fly out." He looked casually up into the sky, which Cirse was about to depart. "If you permit, I will accompany you."

"What is your interest in the affair?" asked Efraim suspiciously.

Lorcas responded with an airy gesture. "I have long wished to visit the Realms. The Rhunes are a fascinating people and I am anxious to learn more about them. And, if the truth be known, I am anxious to pursue one or two acquaintances."

"You might not enjoy your visit. I am Kaiark, but I have enemies and they might not distinguish between us."

"I rely upon the notorious Rhune revulsion against violent conduct, which they abandon only during their incessant wars. And who knows? You might find a companion useful."

"Perhaps. Who is this acquaintance whom you are anxious to cultivate? The Lissolet Sthelany?"

Lorcas nodded glumly. "She is an intriguing young woman; in fact, I will go so far as to say that she represents a challenge. As a rule, pretty ladies find me sympathetic, but the Lissolet Sthelany barely notices my existence."

Efraim gave a sour chuckle. "In Scharrode the situation will be worse rather than better."

"I expect no true triumphs; still, if I can persuade her to alter her expression from time to time, I will consider the journey a success."

"I doubt if all will go so easily. The Rhunes find outland manners coarse and vulgar."

"You are Kaiark; your orders must be obeyed. If you decree tolerance, then the Lissolet Sthelany must instantly bend to your will."

"It will be an interesting experiment," said Efraim. "Well, then, make yourself ready; we leave at once!"

Chapter 6

★ ★ ★

During early isp Efraim arrived at the office of the local air transport service, to find that Lorcas had already hired an aircar of no great elegance—its metalwork stained by long exposure to the elements, the glass of the dome clouded, the flanges around the pods cratered and corroded. Lorcas said apologetically: "It's the best available, and quite dependable; in a hundred and two years the engine has never failed, or so I'm told."

With a skeptical eye Efraim surveyed the vehicle. "If it flies us to Scharrode, I don't care what it looks like."

"Sooner or later the craft will collapse, most likely in mid-air. Still—the alternative is shank's mare along the Fwai-chi trails. The terrain is most impressive, nor would you make so dignified an arrival."

"There is something in what you say," Efraim admitted. "Are you ready to leave?"

"At any time. But let me make a suggestion. Why not send a message ahead to prepare them for your coming?"

"So that someone can fly out and shoot us down?"

Lorcas shook his head. "Aircars are banned to the Rhunes, for just this reason. The present issue is one of dignity, and if I may presume to advise you, a Kaiark announces his arrival so that a formal reception may be arranged. I will speak for you, as your aide, which will lend dignity to the occasion."

"Very well, do as you like."

"The Kraike Singhalissa is now the head of the household?"

"So I would suppose."

At a videophone as antiquated as the aircar, Lorcas put through a call.

A footman in a black and scarlet uniform responded. "I speak for Benbuphar Strang. Please state your business."

"I want a few words with the Kraike Singhalissa," said Lorcas. "I have important information to transmit."

"You must call at some other time. The Kraike is in consultation regarding the investiture."

"Investiture? Of whom?"

"Of the new Kaiark."

"And who will this be?"

"The present Kang Destian, who is next in order of succession."

"And when does the investiture occur?"

In one week's time, when the present Kaiark is to be declared derelict."

Lorcas laughed. "Please inform the Kraike that the investiture may be canceled, since Kaiark Efraim is immediately returning to Scharrode."

The footman stared into the screen. "I cannot take responsibility for such an announcement."

Efraim stepped forward. "Do you recognize me?"

"Ah, Force*, indeed I do!"

"Deliver the message as you heard it from the Noble Matho Lorcas."

"Instantly, Force!" The footman inclined himself in a stiff bow, and faded in a dazzle of halations.

The two returned to the aircar and clambered aboard. Without ceremony the pilot clamped the ports, opened the throttle and the ancient aircraft, creaking and vibrating, lurched up and away to the east.

With the pilot, who identified himself as Tiber Flaussig, talking over his shoulder and ignoring both altimeter and the terrain below, the aircraft cleared the ridges of the First Scarp with a hundred yards to spare. As if by afterthought the pilot lifted the craft somewhat higher, although the land at once fell away a thousand feet to become an upland plain. A hundred sprawling lakes reflected the clouds; scaur and deep-willow grew in isolated copses, with a gnarled catafalque tree here and there. Thirty miles east the Second Scarp thrust crags of naked rock up past the clouds. Flaussig, discussing certain outcrops below, declared them rich sources of such gems as tourmaline, peridot, topaz, and spinel—all protetced from human exploitation by reason of Fwai-chi prejudice. "They claim this as one of their holy places, and so reads the treaty. They care no more for the jewels than for common stones; but they can smell a man from fifty miles away and lay on him their curse of a thousand itches, or a fiery bladder, or piebald skin. The area is now avoided."

Efraim pointed ahead to the looming scarp. "In a

* The term *tsernifer*, here translated as 'Force', refers to that pervasion of psychological power surrounding the person of a kaiark. The word is more accurately rendered as *irresistible compulsion, elemental wisdom, depersonalized force.* The appellative 'Force' is an insipid dilution.

single minute we will all be crushed to pulp, unless you quickly raise this craft at least two thousand feet."

"Ah yes," said Flaussig. "The scarp approaches, and we will give it due respect." The aircar rose at a stomach-gripping rate, and from the engine box came a stuttering wheeze which caused Efraim to twist about in alarm. "Is this vehicle finally disintegrating?"

Flaussig listened with a puzzled frown. "A mysterious sound certainly, one which I have not heard before. Still, were you as old as this vehicle, your viscera would also produce odd noises. Let us be tolerant of the aged."

As soon as the craft once more flew a level course the disturbing sounds dwindled into silence. Lorcas pointed ahead toward the Third Scarp, still fifty miles ahead. "Start now to ascend, in a gradual manner. The aircar is more likely to survive such treatment."

Flaussig acceded to the request, and the vehicle rose at a gradual angle to meet the prodigious bulk of the Third Scarp. Below passed a desolation of ridges, cols, chasms, and, rarely, a small forested valley. Flaussig waved his hand around the fearsome landscape. "Within the range of vision, around the whole of the cataclysmic tumble, live perhaps twenty fugitives: desperadoes, condemned criminals, and the like. Commit no crimes in Port Mar or here is where you will wind up."

Neither Lorcas nor Efraim saw fit to comment.

A cleft appeared; the aircar glided through with rock walls close to right and left and great buffets of wind thrusting the craft from side to side; then the cleft fell away and the aircar flew over a landscape of peaks, cliffs, and river valleys. Flaussig waved his hand in another inclusive arc. "The Realms, the glorious Realms! Beneath us now Waierd, guarded by the Soldiers of Silence . . . And now we fly across the realm Sherras. Notice the castle in the lake . . ."

"How far to Scharrode?"

"Yonder, over the crags. That is the answer given to all such questions. Why do you visit a place so dour?"

"Curiosity, perhaps."

"You'll learn nothing from them; they're as tight as stones, like all Rhunes. Below now and behind those great trees is the town Tangwill, home to no more than two or three thousand. The Kaiark Tangissel is said to be insane for women, so he keeps captives in deep dungeons where they don't know whether or not it is mirk, and he visits them during all the periods of the month, except during mirk when he's off on his prowling."

"Nonsense," muttered Efraim, but the pilot paid no heed.

"The great spire to the left is called Ferkus—"

"Up, man, up!" screamed Lorcas. "You're running us into the ridge!"

With a petulant gesture Flaussig jerked the aircraft high, to skim that crag to which Lorcas had made reference; for a period he flew in sullen silence. Below the ground rose and fell, and Flaussig, disdaining further altitude, veered back and forth among crystalline crags, grazed precipices, skirted glaciers and mounds of scree, the better to display his insouciant control over aircraft, landscape, and passengers. Lorcas made frequent expostulations, which Flaussig ignored, and at last guided the aircar down into an irregular valley three to four miles wide and fifteen miles long. At the eastern end a cascade fell two thousand feet into a lake, with nearby the town Esch. Away from the lake flowed a slow river, curving across a meadow and under Benbuphar Strang, then back and forth from pool to pool to the far western end of the valley, where it departed through a narrow gorge.

Near Esch the valley had been tamed to cultivation; the fields were enclosed by dense hedges of bramble berry, as if to hide them from view. In other such fields grazed cattle, while the slopes to either side of the valley were planted as orchards. Elsewhere meadows alternated with forests of banice, white oak, shrack, interstellar yew; through the clear air the foliages—dark green, crimson, sooty ocher, pale green—glowed like colors painted on black velvet. Efraim half-smiled to the fleeting brush to a sudden poignant emotion. Perhaps an exhalation from his occluded memory? Such twinges had been occurring with increasing frequency. He glanced at Lorcas to find him also staring about in wistful wonder. "I have heard how the Rhunes cherish each stone of the landscape," said Lorcas. "The reason is clear. The Realms are small segments of Paradise."

Flaussig, having unloaded the scanty luggage, now stood in an expectant attitude. Lorcas spoke with slow and careful diction. "The fee was prepaid in Port Mar. The management wished to make sure of their money, no matter what else happened."

Flaussig smiled politely. "In circumstances like the present, a gratuity is usually extended."

"Gratuity?" exclaimed Efraim in a passion. "You are lucky to escape a penalty for criminal ineptitude!"

"Further," said Lorcas, "remain here until his Force the Kaiark permits you to leave. Otherwise he will order his secret agent in Port Mar to meet you and break every bone in your body."

Flaussig bowed in a state of injured dignity. "It shall be as you wish. Our firm has built its reputation upon service. Had I known I was transporting grandees of Scharrode, I would have used more formality, since appropriate behavior is also a watchword at our firm."

Lorcas and Efraim had already turned toward Benbuphar Strang, a castle of black stone, umber tile, timber, and stucco, built to the dictates of that peculiar gaunt style typical of the Rhunes. The chambers of the first floor were enclosed by walls thirty feet high, with tall narrow windows, elaborating above into a complicated system of towers, turrets, promenades, bays, balconies, and eyries. This was home, mused Efraim, and this was terrain over which he had walked a thousand times. He looked westward along the valley, across the pools and meadows, past the successive silhouettes of the forests, the colors muted by the haze, until they became purple-gray shadow under the far crags: he had looked across this vista ten thousand times . . . He felt no recollection.

He had been recognized from the town. Several dozen men in black jackets and buff pantaloons hurried forth, with half as many women in gray gauze gowns.

The men, approaching, performed complicated gestures of respect, then came forward, halting at a distance precisely reckoned by protocol.

Efraim asked, "How have things gone during my absence?"

The most venerable of the men responded: "Tragically, Force. Our Kaiark Jochaim was pierced by a Gorget bolt. Otherwise not badly, but not well. There have been doubts and misgivings. From Torre a band of warriors invaded out land. The Kang Destian ordered out a force, but there was little correspondence in rank*; and no great combat ensued. Our blood

* Rhune warfare is controlled by rigid convention. Several types of engagement are recognized. In formal combat, fighting occurs between persons of equal rank. If a person of high caste attacks one of low caste, the low-caste person may protect, retreat, or retaliate. If a low-caste person attacks a person of high caste, he is reprimanded by everyone. The weapons employed are swords, used only for thrusting, and lances.

On occasion the raiders come masked; they are then known as "mirk-men" and treated as bandits. All weapons may be legitimately used against mirk-men, including the so-called "bore," which propels a short arrow or bolt by means of an explosive charge.

Occasionally large-scale battles occur, when the total manpower of one Realm is mobilized against that of another.

Warriors trained to the use of sky-sails command special prestige. The rules of sky-fighting are even more complex than those governing warfare afoot.

boils for revenge upon Gosso of Gorgetto. The Kang Destian has delayed retaliation; when will he order forth our power? Remember, from the crest of Haujefolge our sails command his castle. We can invade them while Gosso sweats and wheezes, we can drop down a force and take Gorgance Strang."

"First things first," said Efraim. "I now go to Benbuphar Strang to discover what irregularities, if any, exist. Have you information, or even suspicions, in this regard?"

The sage performed another gesticulation of a ritual effacement. "I would never reflect upon Benbuphar irregularities, let alone give them voice."

"Do so now," said Efraim. "You will be doing your Kaiark a service."

"As you will, Force, but remember, by the nature of things, we of the town know nothing. Uncharitable persons blink askance at the Kraike Singhalissa's projected trisme with Kaiark Rianlle of Eccord."

"What?" exclaimed Efraim. "And how is it to be with the Kraike Dervas?"

"She is to be rusticated, or so goes the rumor. Such is Singhalissa's price for the Dwan Jar, when Rianlle yearns to build a pavilion. This at least is common knowledge. We learn also of trisme between the Kang Destian and the Lissolet Maerio. If these trismes were to take place, what then? Does it not seem that Rianlle would sit high in the counsels of Scharrode? Still, now that you are at hand, and Kaiark by right, the question is moot."

"I am pleased with your candor," said Efraim. "What else has occurred during my absence?"

"Nothing of consequence, although, in my opinion, the mood of the realm has become slack. Loons and villains wander by mirk, instead of remaining at home to guard their households; and then when light returns, we are reluctant to unbolt our doors, for fear of finding a corpse on the porch. Again, now that you are home, the evil influences must subside."

He bowed and withdrew; Efraim and Lorcas proceeded across the commons toward the castle, after first dismissing the sullen Flaussig and sending him back to Port Mar.

As they approached, a pair of heralds appeared on the twin bartizans over the portal; lifting coiled bronze sad-horns they blew a set of agitated fanfares. The portals swung wide; a platoon of guards stood at attention, and out marched four heralds playing further fanfares: wild excited progressions of sounds, just perceptibly contrapuntal.

Efraim and Lorcas passed through a vaulted tunnel into a courtyard. In a tall-backed chair sat the Kraike Singhalissa; beside her stood the Kang Destian, dark eyebrows lowering.

The Kraike rose to her feet, to stand almost as tall as Destian; she was a woman of obvious force, with lustrous eyes and angular features. A gray turban contained her dark hair; her gray gauze gown seemed dull and characterless until the eye took note of the subtle play of light, the shadow of the half-concealed figure.

Singhalissa spoke in a high sweet voice: "We give you a ritual welcome, although you have returned at an inconvenient time; why should we deny it? In less than a week the legitimacy of your tenure would have dissolved, as certainly you have instructed yourself. It seems far from civil that you have neglected to notify us of your plans, inasmuch as we have providently taken steps to transfer the succession."

"Your points are well-taken," said Efraim. "I could not dispute them if they were not founded upon incorrect premises. I assure you that my difficulties have far exceeded yours. Nevertheless, I am sorry that you have been inconvenienced and I sympathize with Destian's disappointment."

"No doubt," said Destian. "May we inquire the circumstances of your long absence?"

"Certainly; you are entitled to an explanation. At Port Mar I was drugged, placed aboard a spaceship, and sent far off across the Cluster. I encountered many difficulties and succeeded in returning to Port Mar only yesterday. As soon as possible I hired an aircar and was conveyed to Scharrode."

Destian's mouth compressed even deeper at the corners. He shrugged and turned away.

"Most curious," said Singhalissa, in her high clear voice. "Who worked this malignant deed?"

"I will discuss the matter with you in detail, at some future time."

"As you please." She inclined her head toward Lorcas. "And who is this gentleman?"

"I wish to present my friend, the Noble Matho Lorcas. He has given me invaluable assistance and will be our guest. I believe that he and the Kang Destian became casually acquainted at Port Mar."

Destian scrutinized Lorcas a brief three seconds. Then, muttering something under his breath, he turned away. Lorcas said gravely, "I recall the occasion perfectly; it is a pleasure to renew the acquaintance."

At the back of the colonnade, in the shadow of one of the tall portals, the form of a young woman seemed gradually to materialize. Efraim saw her to be the Lissolet Sthelany, slight and supple in her nimbus of translucent gray gauze. Her eyes, like those of the Kraike, were somber and lustrous, but her features were pensive rather than minatory, delicate rather than crisp, and only remotely similar to those of either Singhalissa or Destian. She was further differentiated by her expression of detachment and indifference. Efraim and Lorcas both might have been strangers for all the animation of her greeting. Lorcas had found Sthelany fascinating at Port Mar, and his interest, so

Efraim noticed, had not diminished—almost too obviously, although no one troubled to take note.

Singhalissa, sensing Sthelany's presence, spoke over her shoulder. "As you see, the Kaiark Efraim is again with us. He has suffered outrageous indignities; some unknown person has played him a series of malicious tricks."

Efraim had been listening with a sour grin. "I can dismayed to hear this. Still, one cannot expect to roam the back alleys of Port Mar and evade the consequences. As I recall, he was in the most questionable company."

"We are all disturbed by the situation," said Singhalissa. "The Kaiark of course has our sympathy. He has brought as his guest the Noble Matho Lorcas, or so I believe his name to be: his friend from Port Mar."

The Lissolet's acknowledgment of the introduction, if any less emphatic, would have been undetectable. She spoke to Efraim in a voice as clear and sweet as that of Singhalissa, "Who performed these heartless acts upon you?"

Singhalissa answered for Efraim. "The Kaiark prefers not to enlarge upon the matter at this time."

"But we are most interested! These indignities offend us all!"

"That is true enough," said the Kraike.

Efraim had been listening with a sour grin. "I can tell you very little. I am as puzzled as you are—perhaps more so."

"More so? I know nothing."

The Kraike said abruptly, "The Kairk and his friend have had a fatiguing journey and will wish to refresh themselves." She addressed herself to Efraim. "I assume that you will now occupy the Grand Chambers?"

"It would seem appropriate that I do so."

Singhalissa turned and beckoned to a grizzled heavy-shouldered man who wore, over the black and scarlet Benbuphar livery, a black velvet mantle embroidered in silver and a black velvet tricorn cap. "Agnois, bring a selection of the Kaiark's effects down from the North Tower."

"At once, Your Presence." Agnois the First Chamberlain departed.

The Kraike Singhalissa ushered Efraim along a dim hall hung with portraits of all the dead kaiarks, each, by the urgency of his gaze and the poise of his upraised hand, straining to communicate his wisdom across the ages.

A pair of tall iron-bound doors barred the way, with a gorgon's head of oiled black iron at the center of each; perhaps contrived by a kaiark's cogence.* Singhalissa halted by the doors; Efraim stepped forward to fling them wide but could not discover the mechanism which controlled the latch. Singhalissa said drily, "Allow me," then pressed a boss. The doors swung open.

They entered a long antechamber, or trophy room. Cases lined the walls, displaying curios, collections, artifacts; objects of stone, wood, fired clay, glass; insects preserved in transparent cubes; sketches, paintings, calligraphy; Books of Life, a thousand other volumes and portfolios, monographs unnumbered. A long table occupied the center of the room, on which glowed a pair of lamps in green glass shades. Above the cases portraits of kaiarks and kraikes stared down at those who passed below.

The trophy room opened on a vast high-ceilinged room paneled in wood almost black with age. Rugs patterned in maroon, blue, and black covered the floor; tall narrow windows overlooked the valley.

The Kraike indicated a dozen cases along the wall.

* The word *cogence* is used to express that fervent erudition and virtuosity of the Rhunes.

"These are Destian's belongings; he assumed that he would be occupying these chambers; he is naturally annoyed by the turn of events." She stepped to the wall and touched a button; almost at once Agnois the First Chamberlain appeared. "Yes, Your Presence?"

"Remove the Kang Destian's belongings."

"At once, Presence." He departed.

"How, may I ask, did the Kaiark meet his death?"

The Kraike looked sharply at Efraim. "You have heard nothing of this?"

"Only that he was killed by the Gorgets."

"We know little more. They came as mirk-men and one of them shot a bolt at Jochaim's back. Destian planned a foray of vengeance immediately after his investiture."

"Destian can order a foray whenever he chooses. I will put no hindrance in his way."

"You intend not to participate?" The Kraike's clear voice tinkled with a cool emotion.

"I would be foolish to do so, while there are mysteries to be clarified. Who knows but what I also might die of a Gorget bolt?"

"You must act as your wisdom directs. When you are rested you will find us in the hall. With your permission I will now leave you."

Efraim bowed his head. "I am grateful for your solicitude."

The Kraike departed. Efraim stood alone in the ancient parlor. In the air hung a redolence of leather bookbindings, waxed wood, old fabric, and also a faint mustiness of disuse. Efraim went to look out one of the tall windows, each protected by an iron shutter. The time was green rowan; the light lay wan across the landscape.

He turned away and gingerly began to explore the chambers of the Kaiark. The parlor was furnished with massive pieces, well-worn and not uncomfortable, if somewhat stately and ponderous. At one end of the room cases ten feet tall displayed books of every description. Efraim wondered what had been Jochaim's special virtuosities. For that matter, what had been his own?

In a sideboard he found various flasks of liquor, for the Kaiark's private ingestion. A rack displayed a dozen swords, evidently weapons of fame and glory.

A portal nine feet tall and three feet wide opened into an octagonal sitting room. A segmented glass dome hugh above, flooded the chamber with light. A green rug covered the floor; the wall panels were painted to represent views over Scharrode from several high vantages; the work, no doubt, of some long-dead kaiark who had professed the rendering of painted landscapes. A spiral stairs led aloft to a balcony, which led to an exterior promenade. Across the sitting room a short hall led into the Kaiark's wardrobe. Uniforms and formal dress hung in closets; chests contained shirts and underlinen; on shelves were ranged dozens of boots, shoes, sandals, slippers: all glossy with polish, brushed and burnished. Kaiark Jochaim had been a punctilious man. The personal belongings, the garments and uniforms communicated nothing. Efraim felt uneasy and resentful; why had not these garments long ago been discarded?

A tall door opened on the Kaiark's bed-chamber: a relatively small room plainly furnished; the bed was little more than a cot, with a hard thin mattress. Efraim saw room for change here; he had no present taste for asceticism. A short hall opened first upon a bathroom and watercloset, then upon a small chamber furnished with a table and chair: the Kaiark's refectory. Even as Efraim examined the room a dumbwaiter rumbled up from the cellar kitchens, bringing a tureen of soup, a loaf of bread, a plate of leeks in oil, a quantity of black-brown cheese, and a tankard of beer. The service, as Efraim would learn, was automatic; every hour the collation would be renewed, and the Kaiark never need suffer the embarrassment of calling for food.

Efraim discovered himself to be hungry and ate with good appetite. Returning into the hall, he noted that it continued to a flight of dark winding stairs. A noise from the bedroom attracted his attention. He returned to find a pair of valets removing the garments of the dead Kaiark and arranging in their stead a wardrobe conspicuously less ample: presumably the clothes he had left in his old quarters.

"I go now to bathe," Efraim told one of the valets. "Lay out something suitable for me to wear."

"With haste, Force!"

"Also, remove this bed, and bring in something larger and more comfortable."

"Immediately, Force!"

Half an hour later Efraim inspected himself in the mirror. He wore a gray coat over a white shirt, black breeches, black stockings, and black velvet shoes—garments suitable for informal occasions within the castle. The clothes hung loosely on his body; he had lost weight since the episode at Port Mar.

The stairs at the back of the hall had not yet been explored. He climbed twenty feet to a landing, where he opened a door and looked out into a hall.

He stepped through. The door seemed to be a section of the paneling, invisible when closed. As he stood examining the door and speculating upon its purpose, the Lissolet Sthelany emerged from a chamber at the end of the hall. At the sight of Efraim, she hesitated, then approached slowly, her face averted. The green rays of Cirse, shining from the window at the end of the hall, backlighted her figure; Efraim wondered how he had ever considered the gauze gowns drab. He watched her as she approached, and it seemed that her cheeks became suffused with a faint flush. Modesty? Annoyance? Excitement? Her expression gave no indication as to her feelings.

Efraim stood watching as she drew nearer. Evidently she intended to continue past, without acknowledging his presence. He leaned forward, half of a mind to put his arm around her waist. Sensing his intent, she stopped short and turned him an alarmed glance. No question as to her beauty, thought Efraim; she was enchanting, perhaps the more so for the peculiar Rhune predispositions.

She spoke in a light colorless voice: "Why do you bolt so precipitously from the mirk-hole? Do you intend to startle me?"

"Mirk-hole?" Efraim looked blankly over his shoulder at the passage. "Yes, of course. I had not considered . . ." Meeting her wondering gaze he stopped short. "No matter. Come down to the Grand Chamber, if you will. I would like to talk with you." He held open the door but Sthelany recoiled in amazement.

"Through the mirk-way?" She stared from Efraim to the passage, then gave a cool trill of laughter. "Do you care so little for my dignity?"

"Of course not," Efraim declared hastily. "I am absentminded of late. Let us go by the ordinary route."

"At your convenience, Force." She waited.

Efraim, recalling nothing of the castle's internal plan, reflected a moment, then set off down the corridor in the direction which seemed most logically to lead to the Kaiark's chambers.

Sthelany's cool voice came from behind him. "Does Your Awesome Presence first intend to inspect the tapestry collection?"

Efraim halted and reversed his direction. He walked past the Lissolet without comment and continued to a bend in the hall, which gave upon a foyer. Before him wide stone stairs flanked by heavy balustrades and archaic lamps of wrought iron led down to the main floor. Efraim descended, with the Lissolet coming demurely behind him. With only a second or two of hesitation he headed for the Kaiark's chambers.

He opened the tall doors with the gorgon's heads without difficulty, and ushered Sthelany into the trophy room. He closed the door and pulled a chair away from the table for her use. Giving him her now familiar glance of sardonic perplexity she asked: "Why do you do that?"

"So that you may sit, and hopefully relax, and so that we may talk at our ease."

"But I may not sit in your presence, under the eyes of your ancestors!" She spoke in a mild and reasonable voice. "Do you wish me to suffer a ghost-blight?"

"Naturally not. Let us go into the parlor, where the portraits will not trouble you."

"Again this is most unconventional."

Efraim lost patience. "If you don't care to talk with me, you certainly have my permission to go."

Sthelany leaned gracefully back against the table. "If you order me to talk, I must obey."

"Naturally I will not give such an order."

"What do you wish to talk about?"

"I don't really know. Truth to tell, I am puzzled. I have undergone a hundred strange experiences; I have seen thousands of new faces; I have visited the Connatic's Palace on Numenes . . . Now that I have returned, the customs of Scharrode seem strange."

Sthelany considered the matter. "For a fact you seem a different person. The old Efraim was rigorously correct."

"I wonder . . . I wonder . . ." mused Efraim. He looked up to find Sthelany watching him intently. "So you notice a difference in me?"

"Of course. If I did not know you so well I would

think you a different man—especially in view of your peculiar absentmindedness."

After a moment Efraim said, "I confess to confusion. Remember, I did not realize I was Kaiark until yesterday. And arriving here, I discover an atmosphere of resentment, which is not at all pleasant."

Sthelany showed surprise at Efraim's ingenuousness. "What would you expect? Singhalissa may no longer call herself Kraike; she lacks all legitimate place here at Benbuphar Strang. No less do I and Destian; we all must make plans for dreary old Disbague. We live here at your sufferance. It is a sad turn of events for us."

"I am not anxious that you leave, unless you wish to go."

Sthelany gave an indifferent shrug. "My feelings are of interest only to myself."

"Incorrect. I am interested in your feelings."

Again Sthelany shrugged. "Naturally I prefer Scharrode to Disbague."

"I see. Tell me, what is your recollection of events in Port Mar during those hours before I disappeared?"

Sthelany grimaced. "They were neither edifying nor entertaining. As you will recall, we stayed at the hotel, which was quite decent and proper. You, Destian, Maerio, and I decided to walk through the town to a place called the Fairy Gardens, where we were to watch puppets. All warned us against the vulgarity we were sure to encounter. But we considered outselves indomitably callous and crossed the bridge, some of us not altogether enthusiastically. You asked directions of a typical young man of the place, capricious and hedonistic—in fact, I believe him to be the same person who accompanied you here. He led us to the Fairy Gardens, but the puppets were gone. Your friend, Lorca, or Lortha, whatever his name, insisted on pouring a bottle of wine, so that we should guzzle and gurgle and swell out our intestinal tracts in full view of all. Forgive my language; I can only report the truth. Your acquaintance showed no shame, and riduculed matters of which he knew nothing. While you conversed, quite enthusiastically, as I recall, with the Lissolet Maerio, this Lorca became remarkably familiar with me, and indeed made some utterly witless proposals. Destian and I left the Fairy Gardens. Maerio, however, remained with you. She is really much too tolerant. We returned to the hotel, where the Kaiark Rianlle became quite perturbed. He sent Destian to escort Maerio back to the hotel, which he did, leaving you in the company of your friend."

"And shortly after," said Efraim, "I was drugged and sent off across space!"

"I should ask your friend what he knows of the matter."

"Bah," said Efraim shortly. "Why would he play me such a trick? Somewhere I have gained an enemy, but I cannot suspect Lorcas."

"You have gained many enemies," said Sthelany in her soft sweet voice. "There are Gosso of Gorgetto and Sansevery of Torre, both of whom owe you blood, and both expect your reprisals. The Kraike Singhalissa and the Kang Destian are much disadvantaged by your presence. The Lissolet Maerio suffered from your ebullience at Port Mar; neither she nor the Kaiark Rianlle will readily forgive you. As for the Lissolet Sthelany"—she paused and looked sidelong at Efraim; in someone else he might have suspected coquetry—"I reserve my thoughts for myself alone. But I wonder if I can any longer contemplate trisme with you."

"I hardly know what to say," Efraim muttered.

Sthelany's eyes glowed. "You seem distrait and not at all concerned. Of course, you have dismissed the compact as trivial, or even forgotten it."

Efraim made a lame gesture. "I have become absentminded . . ."

Sthelany's voice trembled. "For reasons beyond my imagination, you seek to wound me."

"No, no! So much has happened; I am truly confused!"

Sthelany inspected him with skeptically raised eyebrows. "Do you remember anything whatever?"

Efraim rose to his feet and started into the parlor, then imagining Sthelany's emotion should he offer her a cordial, returned slowly to the table.

Sthelany watched his every more. "Why have you returned to Scharrode?"

Efraim laughed hollowly. "Where else could I rule a realm and command the obedience of a person as beautiful as yourself?"

Sthelany abruptly stood back, her face pale save for spots of color in her cheeks. She turned to leave the trophy room.

"Wait!" Efraim stepped forward, but the Lissolet shrank back with a slack jaw, suddenly helpless and frightened. Efraim said: "If you were of a mind to trisme, you must have thought well of me."

Sthelany regained her composure. "This does not necessarily follow; and now I must leave."

Swiftly she departed the chamber. Like a wraith she fled down the corridor, across the Great Hall, in and out of a shaft of green light from the star Cirse, and then she was gone.

Efraim signaled Agnois the First Chamberlain. "Take me to the chambers of the Noble Matho Lorcas."

Lorcas had been lodged on the second level of Minot Tower, in rooms of grotesque and exaggerated amplitude. Hoary beams supported a ceiling almost invisible by reason of height and dimness; the walls, which were faced with carved stone plaques—again the product of someone's cogence—showed a thickness of five feet where the four tall windows opened to a view of the northern mountains. Lorcas stood with his back to a fireplace ten feet wide and eight feet high, in which a disproportionately small fire was burning. He looked at Efraim with a rueful grin. "I am not at all cramped, and there is much to be learned in the documents yonder." He indicated a massive case thirty feet long and ten feet high. "I discover dissertations, contradictions, and reconsideration of these same dissertations: and reconsiderations of the contradictions and contradictions of the reconsiderations—all indexed and cross-indexed in the red and blue volumes yonder. I plan to use some of the more discursive reconsiderations for fuel, unless I am furnished a few more sticks for my fire."

The Kraike Singhalissa hoped to awe and quell this flippant Port Mar upstart, so Efraim suspected. "If you are uncomfortable, a change is easily made."

"By no means!" declared Lorcas. "I enjoy the grandeur; I am accumulating memories to last a lifetime. Come join me by this miserable fire. What have you learned?"

"Nothing of consequence. My return has pleased no one."

"And what of your recollections?"

"I am a stranger."

Lorcas ruminated a moment. "It might be wise to visit your old chambers, and examine your belongings."

Efraim shook his head. "I don't care to do so." He dropped into one of the massive chairs and slumped back, legs outthrust across the flags. "The idea oppresses me." He glanced about the walls. "Two or three sets of ears no doubt are listening to our conversation. The walls are shot with mirk-ways." He jumped to his feet. "We had best look into the matter."

They returned to the Kaiark's chambers; Destian's effects had been removed. Efraim touched the button to summon Agnois, who, upon entering, performed a stiff bow, which almost imperceptibly seemed to lack respect. Efraim smiled. "Agnois, I plan many changes at Benbuphar Strang, possibly including new staff. You may let it be known that I am carefully evaluating the conduct of everyone, from top to bottom."

"Very good, Your Force." Agnois, bowing again, displayed considerably more verve.

"In this regard, why have you denied the Noble Lorcas suitable fires? I consider this an incredible failure of hospitality."

Agnois grew pink in the face; his lumpy nose twitched. "I was given to understand, Force—or better to say—in actuality I must plead guilty of oversight. The matter will be repaired at once."

"A moment, I wish to discuss another matter. I presume that you are acquainted with the affairs of the house?"

"Only to the extent which might be considered discreet and proper, Your Force."

"Very well. As you may know I have been victimized in a most mysterious manner, and I intend to get to the bottom of the business. May I, or may I not, rely upon you for total cooperation?"

Agnois hesitated only an instant, then seemed to heave a doleful sigh. "I am at your service, Force, as ever."

"Very good. Now, let me ask you, is anyone overhearing our present conversation?"

"Not to my knowledge, Force." He went on reluctantly: "I suppose that such a possibility might be said to exist."

"Kaiark Jochaim kept an exact chart of the castle, with all its passages and mirk-holes." Efraim spoke at sheer hazard, on the assumption that among so many records and so much careful lore, a detailed chart of the castle's mirk-ways must inevitably be included. "Bring this article to the table; I wish to examine it."

"Very well, Force, if you will furnish a key to the Privy Case."

"Certainly. Where is Kaiark Jochaim's key?"

Agnois blinked. "Perhaps it bides with the Kraike."

"Where might I find the Kraike at this moment?"

"She refreshes herself* in her chambers."

Efraim made an impatient gesture. "Take me there. I wish a word or two with her."

"Force, do you order me to precede you?"

"Yes, lead the way."

Agnois bowed. He swung smartly around, conducted Efraim out into the Great Hall, up the stairs, along a corridor into the Jaher Tower, and halted before a tall door studded with garnets. At Efraim's signal he thrust the central garnet and the door swung wide. Agnois stood aside, and Efraim marched into the foyer of the Kraike's private chambers. A maid appeared, and performed a quick, supple curtsey. "Your orders, Force?"

"I wish an immediate word with Her Presence."

The maid hesitated, then taking fright at Efraim's expression disappeared the way she had come. A minute passed, two minutes. Then Efraim pushed through the door despite a muffled exclamation from Agnois.

He stood in a long sitting room hung with red and green tapestry, furnished with gilt wood settees and tables. Through an opening to the side he sensed movement; he went on swift strides to the portal and so discovered the Kraike Singhalissa at a small cabinet built into the wall, into which at the sight of Efraim she thrust a small object and slammed the door shut.

* The dialect of the Rhunes is rife with delicate ambiguities. The term 'to refresh oneself' is susceptible to several interpretations. In this case it may be supposed that the Kraike indulges herself in a nap.

Swinging about she faced Efraim, eyes glowing in fury. "Your Force has forgotten the niceties of conduct."

"All this to the side," said Efraim, "I desire that you open the cabinet."

Singhalissa's face became hard and gaunt. "The cabinet contains only personal treasures."

Efraim turned to Agnois. "Bring an axe, at once."

Agnois bowed. Singhalissa made an inarticulate sound. Turning to the wall she tapped a concealed button. The door to the cabinet opened. Efraim spoke to Agnois. "Bring what you find to the table."

Agnois gingerly brought forth the contents of the cabinet: several leather portfolios and on top an ornate key of iron and silver, which Efraim took up. "What is this?"

"The key to the Privy Case."

"And this other matter?"

"These are my private papers," declared Singhalissa in a voice of metal. "My contracts of trisme, the birth documents of the Kang and the Lissolet."

Efraim glanced through the portfolios. The first showed an intricate architectural plan. He glanced at Singhalissa who stared back coldly. Efraim signaled to Agnois. "Look through these documents; return to Her Presence the effects she describes. All others, set aside."

Singhalissa settled herself into a chair and sat stiffly. Agnois leaned his heavy back over the table, peering diffidently into the documents. He finished and pushed one group of papers aside. "These concern the personal affairs of the Kraike. The others more properly belong in the Privy Case."

"Bring them along." With the coldest of nods to Singhalissa, Efraim departed the chamber.

He found Matho Lorcas where he had left him, lounging in a massive leather-backed chair, examining a history of the wars between Scharrode and that realm known as Slaunt, fifty miles south. Lorcas put aside the volume and rose to his feet. "What did you learn?"

"About what I expected. The Kraike has no intention of accepting defeat—not quite so easily." Efraim went to the Privy Case, applied the key and threw wide the heavy doors. For a moment he regarded the contents: sheaves of documents, tallies, certificates, handwritten chronicles. Efraim turned away. "One time or another I must examine these. But for now"—he looked across the room to where Agnois stood, stiff and silent as a piece of furniture. "Agnois."

"Yes, Your Force."

"If you feel that you can serve me with single-minded loyalty, you may continue in your present post. If not, you may resign at this moment, without prejudice."

Agnois spoke in a soft voice: "I served Kaiark Jochaim many years; he discovered no fault with me. I will continue to serve the rightful Kaiark."

"Very good. Find suitable materials and prepare a sketch of Benbuphar Strang, indicating the chambers used by the various members of the household."

"At once, Force."

Efraim went to the massive central table, seated himself, and began to examine the documents he had taken from Singhalissa. He found what appeared to be a ceremonial protocol, certifying the lineage of the House of Benbuphar, beginning in ancient times and terminating with his own name. In crabbed Old Rhune typescript, Kaiark Jochaim acknowledged Efraim, son of the Kraike Alferica, from Cloudscape Castle*, as his successor. A second portfolio contained correspondence between Kaiark Jochaim and Kaiark Rianlle of Eccord. The most recent file dealt with Rianlle's pro-

* Rhune lineage is reckoned through the mother owing to the unregulated circumstances of procreation, although in many cases father and son are mutually aware of their relationship.

posal that Jochaim cede a tract of land known as Dwan Jar, the Whispering Ridge, to Eccord, in consideration of which Rianlle would offer the Lissolet Maerio in trisme to the Kang Efraim. Jochaim politely refused to consider the proposal, stating that trisme between Efraim and Sthelany was under consideration; Dwan Jar could never be relinquished for reasons of which the Kaiark Rianlle was well aware.

Efraim spoke across the table to Agnois. "Why does Rianlle want the Dwan Jar?"

Agnois looked up wonderingly. "For the same reason as always, Force. He would build his mountain eyrie on Point Sasheen, where the way is convenient to and from Belrod Strang. The Kaiark Jochaim, you will remember, refused to indulge the Kaiark Rianlle in his urgent caprice, citing an ancient compact with the Fwai-chi."

"The Fwai-chi? Why should the matter concern them?"

"The Whispering Ridge harbors one of their sanctuaries,* Force." Agnois spoke tonelessly, as if he had decided never again to display surprise at Efraim's vagueness.

"Yes, of course." Efraim opened the third folder and discovered a set of architectural sketches depicting various aspects of Benbuphar Strang. He noticed Agnois averting his gaze in conspicuous disinterest. Here, thought Efraim, were the secret ways of the castle.

The drawings were elaborate and not readily comprehensible. The Kraike might or might not have made copies of this document. At the very least she had pored over the plans in grim fascination; she undoubtedly knew the secret ways as well as she knew the open corridors.

* Inexact translation. More accurately: place of spiritual regeneration, stage of pilgrimage, phase of the life-road.

"That will be all for the moment," Efraim told Agnois. "Under no circumstances discuss our affairs with anyone! If you are questioned, declare that the Kaiark has explicitly forbidden discussion, hints, or intimations of any sort!"

"As you command, Force." Agnois raised his faded blue eyes to the ceiling. "Allow me, Force, if you will, a personal remark. Since the dysfunction of the Kaiark Jochaim, affairs at Benbuphar Strang have not gone altogether well, although the Kraike Singhalissa is, of course, a positive force." He hesitated, then spoke as if the words were forced from his throat by an irresistible inner pressure. "Your return naturally interferes with the plans of the Kaiark Rianlle, and his amicability cannot be taken for granted."

Efraim attempted to seem puzzled and sagacious at the same time. "I have done nothing to antagonize Rianlle—nothing purposeful certainly."

"Perhaps not, but purpose means nothing if Rianlle discovers himself to be thwarted. Effectively, you have annulled the trisme between the Kang Destian and the Lissolet Maerio, and Rianlle will no longer derive profit from a trisme between himself and the Kraike Singhalissa."

"He values the Dwan Jar that highly?"

"Evidently so, Force."

Efraim hardly troubled to dissemble his ignorance. "Might he then attack by force?"

"Nothing can be considered impossible."

Efraim made a sign of dismissal; Agnois bowed and departed.

Isp became umber. Efraim and Lorcas traced, retraced, simplified, coded, and rendered comprehensible the plans to Benbuphar Strang. The passage leading up from the back of the refectory seemed no more than a simple shortcut to the second floor of Jaher Tower. The true mirk-ways radiated from a chamber to the side of the Grand Parlor; passages threaded every wall of the castle, intersecting, opening into nodes, ascending, descending, each coded with horizontal stripes of color, each overlooking chambers, corridors and halls through an assortment of peepholes, periscopes, gratings, and image-amplifiers.

From the chambers of the former Kang Efraim and the current Kang Destian radiated less extensive passages, which could be entered by secret means from the Kaiark's mirk-ways. With a gloomy shiver, Efraim pictured himself in his grotesque man-mask purposefully striding these secret corridors, and he wondered into whose chambers he had thrust wide the door. He pictured the face of the Lissolet Sthelany: pale and taut, her eyes blazing, her mouth half-parted in an emotion she herself would not know how to interpret . . . He returned his attention to the red portfolio, and for the tenth time inspected the index which accompanied it, where the locks and springs controlling each exit were described in detail, together with the alarms intended to thwart illicit passage along the Kaiark's mirk-ways. Exit from the terminal chamber—the so-called "Sacarlatto"—was barred by an iron door, thus protecting the Kaiark from intrusion, and other such doors blocked the passages at strategic nodes.

Efraim and Lorcas, having achieved at least a superficial acquaintance with the maze, rose to their feet and considered the wall of the Grand Parlor. Silence was heavy in the chamber.

"I wonder," mused Lorcas, "I wonder . . . Might someone intend us unpleasantness? A pitfall, or a poison web? Perhaps I am oppressed by the atmosphere. Rhunes, after all, are not allowed to murder—except by mirk."

Efraim made an impatient gesture; Lorcas had accurately verbalized his own mood. He went to the wall, touched a succession of bosses. A panel slid aside; they climbed a flight of stone steps and entered the Sacarlatto. They walked upon a dark crimson carpet, under a chandelier of twenty scintillas. Upon each panel of the black- and red-enameled wainscoting hung a carved marble representation of a man-mask in low relief, so that the object lay near-flat against the panel. Each mask depicted a different distortion; each bore a legend in cryptic symbols. At six stations, mirrors and screens provided views across the Grand Parlor. Lorcas spoke in a hushed voice, which was further attenuated by a quality of the chamber. "Do you smell anything?"

"The carpet. Dust."

"I have a most sensitive nose. I detect a fragrance, an herbal essence."

Standing stiff and white-faced in the gloom, the two men seemed a pair of antique mannequins.

Lorcas spoke again. "The same essence hangs in the air after Singhalissa has passed."

"You believe then that she was here?"

"Very recently—watching us and listening as we worked. Notice, the iron door is ajar."

"We will close it; and now I will sleep. Later we will lock off the other doors and there will be no more prowling and spying."

"Leave this in my hands! I am fascinated by such matters and I am not at all tired."

"As you like. Remember, the Kraike may have set out alarms of her own."

"I will be careful."

Chapter 7

★ ★ ★

In the Kaiark's sleeping chamber, Efraim awoke and lay in the dimness.

On the mantelpiece a clock showed the mode to be aud, with Furad and Maddar about to set and abandon the sky to chill isp. A second dial reported Port Mar Local Time, and Efraim saw that he had slept seven hours—rather longer than he had intended.

He looked up toward the high ceiling, contemplating the condition in which he found himself. His advantages were easily enumerated. He ruled a beautiful mountain realm from a castle of archaic glamour. He had at least partially thwarted his enemy, or enemies; at this moment he, or she, or they, would be brooding long slow thoughts. Benbuphar Strang harbored antagonists, but to what purpose? These persons were at hand when his memory was smothered . . . The thought caused Efraim to shiver with rage and raise up from his couch.

He bathed and took a dismal breakfast of cold meat, bread, and fruit in the refectory. Had he not known the quality of Rhune custom he might have regarded the food as a purposeful affront . . . He speculated as to the advisability of innovation: why should the Rhunes conduct themselves with such exaggerated daintiness when trillions of other folk feasted in public, with never a concern for their alimentary processes? His own single example would only arouse revulsion and censure; he must think further on the matter.

On the racks and shelves of his dressing room he discovered what he took to be his wardrobe of six months before—a somewhat scanty wardrobe, he reflected. He pulled out a mustard-colored tunic with black frogging and dark red lining, and looked it over: a jaunty garment which no doubt on some informal occasion had set off young Kang Efraim to advantage.

Efraim made a soft sound and examined the other garments. He tried to remember the Kaiark Jochaim's wardrobe, at which he had barely glanced, and could only summon an impression of understated elegance, kaiarkal restraint.

Efraim went thoughtfully into the Grand Parlor and summoned Agnois, who seemed uneasy. He shifted his pale blue gaze aside, and as he bowed the fingers of his big white hands kneaded and twisted.

Before Efraim could speak, Agnois said: "Your Force, the Eiodarks of Scharrode wish an audience, as soon as convenient. They will meet you in two hours if that suits Your Force."

"The audience can wait," growled Efraim. "Come along with me." He led Agnois to the dressing room, where he paused and turned a cold stare upon Agnois, causing the chamberlain to blink. "As you know, I have been away from Scharrode a matter of six months."

"Yes, Force."

"I have had many experiences, including an accident which has unfortunately obscured portions of my memory. I tell you this in absolute confidence."

"I will naturally respect this confidence, Your Force," stammered Agnois.

"I have forgotten many small niceties of Rhune custom, and I must rely upon your assistance. For instance, these garments: can this be the whole of my former wardrobe?"

Agnois licked his lips. "No, Your Force. The Kraike made a selection of certain garments; these were then brought here."

"These of course are garments I wore as Kang?"

"Yes, Force."

"They seem somewhat jaunty and extravagant in cut. Do you consider them suitable for a person of my present status?"

Agnois pulled at his pale pendulous nose. "Not altogether, Your Force."

"If I wore these before the eiodarks they would consider me frivolous and irresponsible—a callow young fool, in fact."

"I would suspect as much."

"What precisely were Singhalissa's instructions?"

"She ordered me to transfer these garments; she further suggested that any interference in Your Force's preferences might be considered insolence, both by Your Force and by the Noble Singhalissa herself."

"She told you, in effect, to help me make a fool of myself. Then she summoned the eiodarks to an audience."

Agnois spoke hurriedly: "This is accurate, Force, but—"

Efraim cut him short. "Postpone the audience with the eiodarks. Explain that I must study the events of the last six months. Then remove these garments. Instruct the tailors to prepare me a suitable wardrobe. In the meantime bring here whatever can be salvaged from my old wardrobe."

"Yes, Force."

"Further, inform the staff that the Noble Singhalissa will no longer exert authority. I am bored with these petty intrigues. She is to be known not as the 'Kraike' but as the Wirwove of Disbague."

"Yes, Your Force."

"Finally, Agnois, I am astounded that you failed to notify me of Singhalissa's intentions."

Agnois cried out in frustration: "Force, I intended to obey the Noble Singhalissa's instructions to the letter; but nonetheless, by one means or another, I planned to protect Your Force's dignity. Indeed, you divined the ploy before I had opportunity to alter the situation!"

Efraim gave a curt nod. "Lay out garments at least temporarily appropriate."

Efraim dressed and went out into the Grand Parlor, half-expecting to find Matho Lorcas awaiting him. The room was empty. Efraim stood irresolute a moment, then turned as Agnois entered the chamber. Efraim seated himself in a chair.

"Tell me how the Kaiark Jochaim died."

"Nothing, Force, is surely known. Semaphores warned of mirk-men riding down over the Tassenberg from Gorgetto. The Kaiark sent two troops to attack their flank and led a third force to punish the fore-riders. The mirk-men raced for Suban Forest, then retreated up the defiles toward Horsuke. Suddenly the slopes swarmed with Gorget boremen—the Schardes had been lured into an ambush. Jochaim ordered retreat, and the Scharde warriors fought their way back down the gorge. Somewhere along the way Jochaim took a bolt in his back, and died."

"In the back? Had Jochaim taken flight? This is hard to believe!"

"It is my understanding that he had stationed himself on a knoll where he commanded the disposition of his forces. Evidently a mirk-man had slipped around through the rocks and discharged his bore from the rear."

"Who was he? What was his rank?"

"He was never killed, nor captured, Force. Indeed he was never seen. The Kang Destian assumed command of the troops and brought them safely back into Scharrode; and the folk of both Scharrode and Gorgetto expect that an awful retaliation must take place. Gorgetto is said to be an armed camp."

Efraim, suddenly stifled by his ignorance, pounded his fists upon the arms of his chair. "I feel like the fool in a game of blindman's bluff. I must inform myself; I must learn more of the realm."

"This, Force, may be accomplished without delay; you need merely consult the archives, or if you prefer, the Kaiarkal Pandects along the wall yonder—the volumes in the green and red bindings." Agnois spoke eagerly, relieved that Efraim should be distracted from the episode of the wardrobe.

For three hours Efraim explored the history of Scharrode. Between Gorgetto and Scharrode had existed centuries of strife. Each had dealt the other cruel blows. Eccord had been sometimes an ally, sometimes a foe, but recently had gained greatly in power and now outmatched Scharrode. Disbague occupied a small shadowed valley high in the Gartfang Rakes, and was considered of small consequence, though the Disbs were credited with a dark deviousness, and many of the women were witches.

Efraim reviewed the noble lineages of Scharrode and learned something of trismes which united them with other realms. He read about himself: of his participation in arrays, exercises, and campaigns; he learned that he was considered bold, persistent, and somewhat assertive. In pressing for innovation he seemed often to have been at odds with Jochaim, who insisted upon tradition.

He read of his mother, the Kraike Alferica, who had drowned in a boating accident on Lake Zule during a visit to Eccord. A list of those present at the obsequies included the then Lissolet Singhalissa of Urrue Strang in Disbague. Very shortly thereafter, Jochaim contracted a new trisme and Singhalissa came to live at Benbuphar Strang, along with her children Destian and Sthelany, who were both conceived out of trisme, a circumstance neither unusual nor consequential.

Bloated with facts, Efraim put aside the Pandects and rising to his feet he stretched and slowly paced the Grand Parlor. At a sound he looked up, expecting Matho Lorcas, but found only Agnois. Efraim continued his deliberations. He must reach a decision in connection with the Noble Singhalissa. She had attempted to conceal a number of important documents, then had tried to embarrass and demean him. If he simply adopted a manner of lofty disdain, she would certainly attempt new intrigues. Nonetheless—because of the revulsion which Singhalissa aroused in him—he felt an unconquerable reluctance toward dealing harshly with her; such acts created an intimacy of their own, like that hateful empathy between the torturer and his victim. Still, he must make some sort of response, lest she consider him futile and indecisive.

"Agnois, I have come to a decision. The Noble Singhalissa is to be transferred from her present suite into that now occupied by friend Matho Lorcas. Bring the Noble Lorcas to more congenial quarters in the Jaher Tower. Attend to this at once. I want no delay."

"Your orders shall be carried out! May I venture a comment?"

"Certainly."

"Why not send her back to Disbague? At Urrue Strang she would seem to be at a safe distance."

"The suggestion is sensible. However, she might not remain at Disbague, but set about organizing troubles from all directions. Here, at least, she is under my eye. Again, I do not know that person who dealt me harm six months ago. Why expel Singhalissa until I learn the truth? Also"—Efraim hesitated. If Singhalissa departed, Sthelany almost certainly would depart too, but he did not care to explain as much to Agnois.

He walked up and down the parlor wondering how much Agnois knew of mirk-deeds about the castle, and how much Agnois could tell him in regard to Sthelany. What was her usual conduct during mirk? Did she bolt her door and bar her windows, as fearful maidens were wont to do? Where was Sthelany now? In fact: "Where is Matho Lorcas?"

"He accompanies the Lissolet Sthelany; they walk in the Garden of Bitter Odors."

Efraim grunted and continued his pacing. As he might have expected. He gave Agnois a brusque gesture. "See that the Noble Singhalissa is moved to her new quarters at once. You need supply no explanations; your orders are simple and explicit. No, wait! You may say that I am angry with you for bringing useless old clothes to my wardrobe."

"Very well, Force." Agnois hurried from the chamber. After a moment Efraim followed. Passing through the silent reception hall, he went out upon the terrace. Before him spread the distant landscape, placid in the halcyon light of umber. Matho Lorcas came running up the steps.

"So ho!" cried Lorcas, in what Efraim considered unnatural cheer, or perhaps he was nervously gay. "I wondered how long you intended to sleep."

"I've been awake for hours. What have you been doing?"

"A great deal. I explored passages out of the Sacarlatto. For your information the passages leading to the chambers of both the Noble Singhalissa and the Lissolet Sthelany are obstructed—sealed off with walls of masonry. When mirk arrives, you must turn your attention elsewhere."

"Singhalissa has been busy."

"She overrates the magnetism of her precious body," said Lorcas. "Sthelany is a different matter."

"It appears that you must seduce her by more conventional means," said Efraim in a morose voice.

"Ha hah! I would expect more success chiseling through the masonry. Still, either method is a challenge, and I am stimulated by challenges. What a triumph for the liberal philosophy should I succeed!"

"True. If you want to see how the land lays, why not invite her to take lunch with you?"

"Oh, I know how the land lays. I learned the entire map six months ago in Port Mar. In a certain sense we're old friends."

Agnois stepped forth from the Reception Hall, his lined gray face limp and loose under the velvet tricorn emblematic of his office. He saluted Efraim. "The Noble Singhalissa states that she is most distressed by your orders, and that she finds them incomprehensible."

"You offered her my remark in regard to the wardrobe?"

"I did, Force, and she professed bewilderment. She urges that you condescend to receive her at an inhalation,* in order to discuss the matter."

"Certainly," said Efraim. "In, let us say, two hours, when umber becomes green rowan, if yonder phase-dial is faithful."

"Two hours, Force? She used an urgent form of speech, and evidently wishes the benefit of your wisdom at once."

"I am suspicious of Singhalissa's immediacies," said

* The word *sherdas*, an inexact translation. Those attending a *sherdas* are seated around a table. From properly disposed orifices a succession of aromatic odors and perfumes is released. To praise the fumes too highly, or to inhale too deeply is considered low behavior and leaves the guilty person open to suspicions of gourmandizing.

Efraim. "Two hours will enable you to provide exactly proper garments for me, and for the Noble Matho Lorcas. Additionally, I have certain arrangements to make."

Agnois departed, puzzled and resentful. For the tenth time Efraim wondered as to the advisability of replacing him. With his special knowledge, Agnois was almost indispensable; but Agnois also was given to vacillation and at the mercy of the last personality with whom he had come into contact.

Efraim said to Lorcas: "You would like to attend an inhalation, I take it?"

"Of course. It will be an unforgettable experience—one among many, if I may say so."

"Then meet me in the Grand Parlor in two hours. Your quarters have been changed to the Jaher Tower, incidentally. I am transferring Singhalissa to those you now occupy." Efraim grinned. "I hope to teach her not to play tricks on the Kaiark."

"I doubt if you'll succeed," said Lorcas. "She knows tricks you've never thought of. If I were you I'd look in my bed for snakes before jumping under the covers."

"Yes," said Efraim. "No doubt you are right." He entered the castle, crossed the reception hall, passed along the Corridor of Ancestors, but instead of entering the Trophy Room, turned aside into a corridor paved with brown and white tiles, and so came to a chamber which served as office, bursary, and domestic headquarters. A bench by the side wall supported an ancient communicator.

Efraim closed and locked the door. He addressed himself to the communicator code-book, then pressed a set of discolored old buttons. The screen glowed with pale light, showing sudden jagged disks of carmine red as the summons sounded at the opposite end of the connection.

Three or four minutes passed. Efraim sat patiently.

To expect a crisp response would have been unrealistic.

The screen glowed green, powdered into fugitive dots which reformed to display the visage of a pale old man with locks of lank white hair dangling past his ears. He peered at Efraim with a half-challenging, half-myopic glare and spoke in a rattling croak. "Who calls Gorgance Strang, and for what purpose?"

"I am Efraim, Kaiark of Scharrode. I wish to speak with your master the Kaiark."

"I will announce that Your Force awaits him."

Another five minutes passed, then upon the screen appeared a massive copper-colored face from which hung a great beak of a nose and a deep pendulum of a chin. "Kaiark Efraim, you have returned to Scharrode. Why do you call me, when no such communication has occurred for a hundred years."

"I call you, Kaiark Gosso, for knowledge. While I was absent, mirk-men from Gorgetto entered Scharrode. During this raid the Kaiark Jochaim suffered death from a Gorget bolt, which burst open his back."

Gosso's eyes contracted to ice-blue slits. "So much may be fact. What then? We await your onslaught. Send over your mirk-men; we will impale them on ridgeline saplings. Marshal your noblemen, advance upon us with open faces. We will face you rank for rank and slaughter the best of Scharrode."

"I did not call to inquire the state of your emotions, Gosso. I am not interested in rhodomontade."

Gosso's voice became profoundly deep. "Why, then, have you called?"

"I find the circumstances of Kaiark Jochaim's death peculiar. In the melée of mirk-men and Scharde troops, he commanded from the rear. Did he turn his back to the flight? Unlikely. So then, who among your mirk-men killed the Scharde Kaiark?"

"No one has asserted such a triumph," rumbled Gosso. "I made careful inquiry, to no avail."

"A provocative situation."

"From your point of view, indeed." Gosso's eyelids relaxed slightly; he moved back into his chair. "Where were you during the raid?"

"I was far away—at Numenes and the Connatic's Palace. I have learned many new things, and one of them is this—the raids and onslaughts between Gorgetto and Scharrode amount to mutual catastrophe. I propose a truce."

Gosso's ropy mouth drew back to display his teeth, not a grin, so Efraim presently realized, but a grimace of reflection.

"What you say is true enough," said Gosso at last. "There are few old men either in Gorgetto or Scharrode. Still, everyone must die sooner or later, and if the warriors of Gorgetto are denied the raiding of Scharrode, how will I keep them occupied?"

"I have troubles of my own. No doubt you can find a way."

Gosso cocked his head to the side. "My warriors may protest such an insipid existence. The raids drain their energies, and life is easier for me."

Efraim said shortly: "You can notify those who question your authority that I am resolved to end the raids. I can offer honorable peace; or I can assemble all my forces and totally destroy Gorgetto. As I study the Pandects I see that this is within my capabilities, if at the cost of many lives. Most of these many lives will be Gorget, inasmuch as we command the heights with our sails. It appears to me that the first choice makes the fewest demands upon everybody."

Gosso gave a sardonic caw of laughter. "So it might appear. But never forget we have rejoiced in the slaughter of Schardes for a thousand years. In Gorgetto a boy does not become a man until he kills his Scharde. Still, you seem to be serious and I will consider the matter."

The Salon of Sherdas and Private Receptions occupied the third level of the squat Arjer Skyrd Tower. Instead of the modestly proportioned chamber Efraim had expected, he found a hall seventy feet long and forty feet wide, with a floor of black and white marble blocks. Six tall windows admitted floods of that curious olive-green light characteristic of umber passing into green rowan. Marble pilasters broke the wall into a series of bays, color-washed a pale russet. In each stood a massive urn three feet tall carved from black-brown porphyry; the product of a cogence. The urns contained white sand and plumes of dry grass, without odor. A table ten feet wide and twenty feet long supported four etiquette screens. At each side of the table a chair had been placed.

Agnois hurried forward. "Your Force has arrived a trifle early; our arrangements, I fear to say, are incomplete."

"I came early intentionally." Efraim inspected the chamber, then the table. He asked in a soft voice: "The Kaiark Jochaim frequented this salon?"

"Indeed, Force, when the company was not numerous."

"Which place was reserved for him?"

"Yonder, Force, is the Kaiark's place." Agnois indicated the far side of the table.

Efraim, now accustomed to the unconscious signals which indicated Agnois' moods, eyed him attentively. "That is the chair used by Kaiark Jochaim? It is precisely like the others; they are identical."

Agnois hesitated. "These are the chairs ordered out by the Noble Singhalissa."

Efraim controlled his voice with an effort. "Did I not instruct you to disregard Singhalissa's orders?"

"I recall something of the sort, Force," said Agnois lamely, "but I tend to obey her by reflex, especially in small matters such as this."

"Do you consider this a small matter?"

Agnois grimaced and licked his lips. "I had not analyzed it along such lines."

"But the chair is not that chair customarily used by the Kaiark?"

"No, Your Force."

"In fact, it is a chair quite unsuitable to the dignity of a Kaiark—especially under the present conditions."

"I suppose that I must agree with you, Force."

"So again, Agnois, you have at worst conspired, at best cooperated, with Singhalissa in her attempts to make me a buffoon and so diminish my authority."

Agnois uttered a cry of anguish. "By no means, Force! I acted in all innocence!"

"Set the table to rights, instantly!"

Agnois turned a side-look toward Lorcas. "Shall I seat five, Your Force?"

"Leave it at four."

The offending chair was removed; another more massive, inlaid with carnelians and turquoises, was brought in. "Notice, Force," said Agnois effusively, "the small mesh here by your ear, by which the Kaiark can receive messages and advice."

"Very good," said Efraim. "I will expect you to stand in concealment and advise me as to etiquette and custom."

"With pleasure, Your Force!"

Efraim seated himself and placed Lorcas at the end of the table to his right.

Lorcas said reflectively: "These tricks are really rather petty—not what one might expect of Singhalissa."

"I don't know what to expect from Singhalissa. I imagine that her aim is to demonstrate me a fool as well as an amnesiac, so that the eiodarks will eject me in favor of Destian."

"You'd do well to pack her off."

"I suppose so. Still—"

Singhalissa, Sthelany, and Destian entered the chamber; Efraim and Lorcas politely rose to their feet. Singhalissa came a few steps forward, then halted, regarding the two remaining chairs with pinched nostrils. She then spared a quick glance for the stately chair which Efraim occupied. "I am somewhat baffled," she said. "I envisioned an informal discussion, in which all opinions might most expeditiously be aired."

Efraim replied in an even voice: "I could not conceive a conference on a basis other than propriety. But I am surprised to see the Squire Destian; from the arrangements I understood that only you and the Noble Sthelany planned to attend our conference. Agnois, be so good as to arrange another place there, to the left of Her Dignity the Wirwove. Sthelany, be so good as to seat yourself in this chair to my left."

Smiling a faint vague smile, Sthelany took her seat. Singhalissa and Destian stood aside with dour faces as Agnois rearranged the table. Efraim watched Sthelany surreptitiously, as always wondering what went on in her brain. At this moment she seemed indolent, careless, and totally introverted.

Singhalissa and Destian at last were seated; Efraim and Lorcas gravely returned to their own places. Singhalissa made a small movement, but Lorcas gave a peremptory rap on the table with his knuckles, causing Singhalissa and Destian to look at him questioningly. Sthelany was studying Efraim with an interest almost embarrassingly intent.

Efraim spoke. "The present circumstances are strained, and certain of you have been forced to accept an attenuation of prospects. In reference to the events of the last six months, I remind you that I have been the chief victim. Excepting, of course, the Kaiark Jochaim, who was robbed of his life. Nevertheless, the inconveniences I personally have suffered have made me callous of lesser complaints, and it is on this basis that we hold our discussion."

Sthelany's smile became even more vague; Destian's sneer was almost audible. Singhalissa gripped the arms of her chair with long fingers, so tightly that bones shone luminous through the skin. Singhalissa replied: "Needless to say, we all must adapt to changing circumstances; it is sheer futility to do otherwise. I have conferred long and earnestly with the Noble Destian and the Lissolet Sthelany; we all are perplexed by your misfortunes. You have been a victim of unconventional violence,* which I understand is not uncommon at Port Mar." Singhalissa's flick of a glance toward Lorcas was almost too swift to be sensed. "You were doubtless waylaid by some off-worlder, for reasons beyond my comprehension."

Efraim grimly shook his head. "This theory commands low probability, especially in view of certain other facts. I was almost certainly beset by a Rhune enemy, for whom our standards of decency have lost all meaning."

Singhalissa's high sweet voice became a trifle strident. "We cannot evaluate undisclosed facts, but in any event your enemy is unknown to us. I only wonder if, after all, there has not been a mistake."

For the first time Lorcas spoke. "To clarify matters once and for all, are you giving His Force to understand that in the first place, none of you have knowledge of the event at Port Mar, and secondly, that none of you have received information regarding this event, and thirdly, that none of you can guess who might be responsible?"

No one answered. Efraim said gently: "The Noble

* An act of molestation or violence—a mirk-deed, so to speak—committed during the daylight hours, a depravity unimaginable among persons of dignity.

Matho Lorcas is my friend and counselor; his question is a fair one. What of you, Squire Destian?"

Destian responded in a surly baritone: "I know nothing."

"Lissolet Sthelany?"

"I know nothing of anything."

"Your Dignity the Wirwove?"

"The affair is incomprehensible."

Through the mesh at the back of Efraim's chair sounded Agnois' hoarse whisper. "It would be politic to ask Singhalissa if she might care to refresh herself and the company with a medley of vapors."

Efraim said: "I naturally accept your explicit assurances. If anyone chances to recall some forgotten fact which may be relevant, I will be grateful to hear it. Perhaps we should now entreat Her Dignity to refresh us with vapors."

Singhalissa leaned stiffly forward and drew out a panel in front of her, displaying knobs, toggles, bulbs and other mechanisms, then drawers to right and left containing hundreds of small vials. Her long fingers worked with intricacy and deftness. Vials were lifted; drops of liquid poured into a silver orifice were followed by powders and a gout of seething green liquor. Then she pushed a button and a pump blew the fumes along tubes under the table and up behind the etiquette screens. Meanwhile, with her left hand, Singhalissa was altering her first vapor so that it might modulate into a second which she was busy preparing with her right hand.

The fumes followed each other like musical tones, and ended, as with a coda, upon an artfully bitter nose-wrenching whiff.

Agnois' whisper sounded in Efraim's ear. "Call for more; this is etiquette!"

Efraim said: "Your Dignity has only stimulated our expectations; why must you stop now?"

"I am flattered that you honor my efforts." But Singhalissa sat back from the vials.

After a pause Destian spoke, a saturnine half-smile trembling on his lips. "I am curious to learn as to how you intend to punish Gosso and his jackals."

"I will take counsel upon the matter."

Singhalissa, as if impelled by an irresistible creative urge, once more bent over the vials; again she poured and vapors issued from behind the etiquette screens. In Efraim's ear sounded Agnois' husky whisper: "She is discharging raw essences at random, concocting a set of stinks. She understands your distrait condition and hopes to draw forth fulsome compliments."

Efraim leaned back from the etiquette screen. He glanced at Destian who could scarcely control his merriment. Sthelany sat with a wry expression. Efraim said: "Her Dignity the Wirwove suddenly seems to have lost her sure instincts. Some of these vapors are absolutely amazing, even for the entertainment of a group as informal as this. Perhaps Her Dignity attempts a set of new combinations imported from Port Mar?"

Singhalissa wordlessly desisted from her manipulations. Efraim sat erect in his chair. "The subject we had not yet touched upon was my order to move Your Dignity to Minot Tower. In view of the chairs and the fumes, I will not reconsider my decision. There has been altogether too much interference and meddling. I hope that we have seen the last of it, inasmuch as I would not care to inconvenience Your Dignity to an even greater extent."

"Your Force is most considerate," said Singhalissa, without so much as a quiver in her voice.

Through the tall windows the light had changed, as umber fully gave way to green rowan, with Cirse barely grazing the horizons.

Sthelany said: "Mirk approaches; dark hideous mirk

when the gharks and hoos come forth and all the world is dead."

Lorcas asked in a cheerful voice: "What is a ghark and who is a hoo?"

"Evil beings."

"In human form?"

"I know nothing of such things," said Sthelany. "I take refuge behind a door triple-bolted and strong iron shutters at my windows. You must ask elsewhere for your information."

Matho Lorcas gave his head a shake of whimsical wonder. "I have traveled far and wide," he said, "and never cease to be amazed by the diversities of Alastor Cluster."

The Lissolet Sthelany half-yawned, then spoke in easy voice: "Does the Noble Lorcas include the Rhunes among those peoples who excite his amazement?"

Lorcas grinned and leaned forward. Here was the milieu he loved: conversation! Supple sentences, with first and second meanings and overtones beyond, outrageous challenges with cleverly planned slip-points, rebuttals of elegant brevity; deceptions and guiles, patient explanations of the obvious, fleeting allusions to the unthinkable. As a preliminary, the conversationalist must gauge the mood, the intelligence, and the verbal facility of the company. To this end a few words of pedantic exposition often proved invaluable. "By an axiom of cultural anthropology, the more isolated a community, the more idiosyncratic become its customs and conventions. This of course is not necessarily disadvantageous.

"On the other hand, consider a person such as myself: a rootless wanderer, a cosmopolitan. Such a person tends to flexibility; he adapts himself to his surroundings without qualms or misgivings. His baggage of conventions is simple and natural, the lowest common denominator of his experience. He evinces a kind of universal culture which will serve him almost anywhere across Alastor Cluster, throughout the Gaean Reach. I make no virtue of this flexibility, except to suggest that it is more comfortable to travel with than a set of conventions, which, if jostled, work emotional strains upon those who espouse them."

Singhalissa joined the conversation, speaking in a voice as dry as the rustle of dead leaves. "The Noble Lorcas with earnest conviction proposes a view which I fear we Rhunes regard as banal. As he knows, we never travel, except rarely to Port Mar. Even were we disposed to travel, I doubt if we would school ourselves in habits which we find not only vulgar but repellent. This is an informal gathering; I will venture upon an unpleasant topic. The ordinary citizen of the Cluster shows a lack of self-consciousness regarding his bowel which is typically animal. Without shame he displays his victual, salivates, wads it into his orifice, grinds it with his teeth, massages it with his tongue, impels the pulp along his intestinal tract. With only little more modesty he excretes the digested mess, occasionally making jokes as if he were proud of his alimentary facility. Naturally we obey the same biological compulsions, but we are more considerate of our fellows and perform these acts in privacy." As she spoke Singhalissa never abandoned her mordant monotone.

Destian uttered a soft chuckle endorsing her views.

Lorcas however would not be daunted. He nodded sagely. "Everything depends upon the quality of one's conventions. Agreed! But we must examine this so-called quality for its usefulness. Overcomplicated, overstrict conventions limit a person's life-options. They confine his mind and stunt his perceptions. Why, in the name of the Connatic's pet owl, should we even consider a limit to the possibilities of this, our one and single life?"

"You will confuse us all if you talk in ultimates and eschatologies," said Singhalissa with a cold smile. "They are not germane in any case. One may exemplify any point of view, no matter how absurd, by carefully citing an appropriate, or even an artificial, theory. The traveler and cosmopolitan whom you have chosen as your paladin above all else should realize the difference between abstractions and living human beings, between sociological concepts and durable communities. As I listen to you I hear only ingenuousness and didactic theory."

Lorcas compressed his lips. "Perhaps because you are hearing views which contradict your emotions. But I stray from the mark. The durable communities you mention are beside the point. Societies are amazingly tolerant of abuse, even those burdened with dozens of obsolete or unnatural or even baneful conventions."

Singhalissa allowed herself to show open amusement. "I suspect that you take an extreme position. Only children are intolerant of conventions. They are indispensable to an organized civilization, like discipline to an army, or foundations to a building, or landmarks to a traveler. Without conventions civilization is a handful of water. An army without discipline is a mob. A building without foundations is rubble. A traveler without landmarks is lost."

Lorcas stated that he opposed not all convention, but only those which he found irksome and pointless.

Singhalissa refused to let him off so easily. "I suspect that you refer to the Rhunes, and here, as a stranger, you are particularly handicapped in your judgments. I find my way of life orderly and reasonable, which should certainly satisfy you. Unless, of course, you consider me undiscriminating and stupid?"

Lorcas saw that he had caught a Tartar. He shook his head. "By no means! Quite the contrary. Without hesitation I agree that, at the very least, your outlook upon life is different from mine."

Singhalissa had already lost interest in the conversation. She turned to Efraim. "With your permission, Force, I take my leave."

"As you wish, Your Dignity."

Singhalissa stalked from the room in a flutter of gray gauze, followed by Destian, stiff and erect, and then, Sthelany. Behind marched Efraim and Matho Lorcas, somewhat subdued. They found themselves on the arcade which connected the third level of Arjer Skyrd to the high parlors of the North Tower, then gave upon the upper balcony of the herbarium.

Descending the North Tower staircase, they were arrested by a sudden clanging of gongs, followed by a wild braying of horns in an agitated fanfare.

Singhalissa glanced back over her shoulder; her thin cheeks were compressed into an unmistakable smile.

Chapter 8

★ ★ ★

Efraim continued down the staircase to the frenzy of the fanfare produced by six men with convolved bronze sad-horns. Six horns, wondered Efraim? He himself, the returning Kaiark, had only been greeted with four! A slight which he had failed to notice.

The front portals had been flung ajar, and here stood Agnois, wearing a long white cloak crusted over with blue and silver embroidery and a complicated turban-like headdress: garments reserved for the most profoundly serious occasions. Efraim compressed his lips. What to do with the wretched Agnois, who had assisted him during the reception, but who had failed to warn him of whatever now was about to ensue?

The fanfare became a hysteria of yelling horns, to halt abruptly as a man in splendid black garments, picked out with pink and silver stripes, strode through the portal. Behind him marched four eiodarks. All wore headgear of pink and black cloth, wound up on pronged fillets of silver.

Efraim halted a moment on the landing, then descended slowly. Agnois cried out: "His Majestic Force, the Kaiark Rianlle of Eccord!"

Rianlle halted, scrutinizing Efraim with pale hazel eyes under dark golden eyebrows. He stood stiffly erect, aware of the splendid spectacle he made: a man in the fullest vigor of his life, not yet middle-aged, square-faced, with curling dark golden hair; a man of pride and passion, perhaps lacking in humor, but certainly not a person to be taken lightly.

Efraim stood waiting until Rianlle advanced another two steps. Efraim said: "Welcome to Benbuphar Strang. I am pleased, if surprised, to see you."

"Thank you." Rianlle turned abruptly away from Efraim and performed a formal bow. Down the stairs came Singhalissa, Destian, and Sthelany.

Efraim said: "You are of course well-acquainted with her Dignity the Wirwove, the Squire Destian, and the Lissolet Sthelany. This is the Noble Matho Lorcas, of Port Mar."

Rianlle acknowledged the introduction by no more than a cold glance. Matho Lorcas bowed courteously. "At your service, Force."

Efraim stepped aside and signaled to Agnois. "Conduct these noble gentlemen to appropriate chambers where they may refresh themselves, then come to the Grand Parlor."

Agnois presently appeared in the Grand Parlor. "Yes, Your Force?"

"Why did you not notify me that Rianlle was to arrive?"

Agnois spoke in an injured voice: "I did not know myself, until Her Dignity upon leaving the salon ordered me to prepare a reception. I barely had time to accomplish the task."

Efraim said, "I see. He wears his headgear in the castle; is this customary and polite?"

"It is formal usage, Force. The headdress signifies authority and autonomy. In a formal colloquy of equals both parties will dress similarly."

"Bring me suitable garments and headgear, if any are available."

Efraim dressed. "Conduct Rianlle here whenever he is so minded. If his retinue starts to come, explain that I prefer a private discussion with Rianlle."

"As you wish, Force." Agnois hesitated. "I might point out that Eccord is a powerful realm with victorious traditions. Rianlle is a vain man but not stupid. He esteems himself and his prestige at an exalted level."

"Thank you, Agnois. Bring in Rianlle; I will deal with him as carefully as possible."

Half an hour later Agnois ushered Rianlle into the Parlor. Efraim rose to greet him. "Will you sit? Those chairs are quite comfortable."

"Thank you," Rianlle settled himself.

"Your visit is of course most welcome," said Efraim. "You will forgive me if I seem disorganized; I have hardly had time to collect my wits."

"You returned at a most opportune moment," observed Rianlle, his hazel eyes wide and luminous. "At least for yourself."

Efraim sat back in his chair and inspected Rianlle a full five seconds. Then he said in a cool unaccented voice: "I did not time my return on this basis; I was unaware that Jochaim had been murdered until my arrival in Port Mar."

"Allow me to offer my personal condolences and those of all Eccord upon this untimely death. Did you use the word murder?"

"The evidence indicates something of the sort."

Rianlle nodded slowly and looked thoughtfully across the room. "I came both to express my sympathy and to consolidate the friendly relations between our realms."

"You may take for granted my desire that they continue."

"Excellent. I assume that you intend a smooth continuity between the policies of Jochaim and your own?"

Efraim began to sense a pressure behind Rianlle's suave remarks. He said cautiously: "In many cases, no doubt this will be true. In others, the simple mutability of life and circumstance dictates changes."

"A prudent and flexible point of view! Allow me to offer my commendation! In the relations between Eccord and Scharrode there will be no mutability; I would like to assure you that I intend to honor to the letter every commitment made by me to Jochaim; I would like to hear that the converse holds true."

Efraim made an affable gesture. "Let us not talk of all the facts and anything I could now say would be tentative. But since our two realms are so closely knit in amity, what benefits one benefits the other, and you may be assured that I intend to do my best for Scharrode."

Rianlle glanced sharply at Efraim, then stared toward the ceiling. "Agreed; large matters may wait. There is one rather inconsequential issue which we can easily resolve now without prejudice to your program. I refer to that trifle of territory along Whispering Ridge where I wish to build a pavilion for our mutual enjoyment. Jochaim was on the point of signing the parcel over to me when he met his death."

"I wonder if there was any connection between the two events," mused Efraim.

"Of course not! How could there be?"

"My imagination is overactive. In regard to Whispering Ridge I must admit an aversion toward yielding so much as a square inch of our sacred Scharrode soil; still, I will study the matter."

"Not satisfactory!" Rianlle's voice had taken on an edge, and sang like a vibrating wire. "I am thwarted in my wishes!"

"Is anyone ever continually and completely gratified? Let us talk no more of the subject. Perhaps I can induce the Lissolet to contrive a series of stimulating atmospheres . . ."

At the great twenty-sided table in the Formal Reception Chamber, Rianlle sat stiff and glum. Sthelany formulated a series of fumes, somehow suggesting a walk over the hills—soil and sunlit vegetation, water and wet rocks, the perfume of anthion and wood violet, mold, rotten wood, and camphor. She worked without Singhalissa's deftness, rather seeming to amuse herself among the vials as a child might play with colored chalks. Sthelany's fingers began to move faster; she had become interested in her contrivances as a musician suddenly perceives meanings in his music which he is forced to explicate. Gone was the hillside, away the forest; the vapors were at first gay, tart, and light; gradually they lost character, only to become sweetly melancholic, like heliotrope in a forgotten garden. And this odor in turn became pervaded with a bitter exudation, then a salt pungency, then a final despairing black reek. Sthelany looked up with a twisted smile and closed the drawers.

Rianlle uttered an ejaculation: "You have performed with enormous artistry; you have shaken us all with cataclysmic visions!"

Efraim looked around the table. Destian sat toying with a silver bracelet; Singhalissa sat stiff and staring; the eiodarks of Eccord muttered together. Lorcas stared in wonder toward Sthelany. Efraim thought: he is totally fascinated, but he had better make his emotion less overt, or he will be accused of sebalism.

Rianlle turned to Efraim. "When you said murder, you used an inglorious word to describe the death of the honored Jochaim. How then will you deal with that dog Gosso?"

Efraim held his face immobile against a surge of annoyance. He had used the word murder perhaps indiscreetly; but need Rianlle blurt out the details of what Efraim had considered a confidential conversation? He felt the sudden interest of both Singhalissa and Destian.

"I have made no precise plans. I plan to end the war with Gorgetto on one basis or another; it is useless and it bleeds us white."

"If I understand you correctly, you intend to prosecute only useful wars?"

"If wars there must be, I intend to fight for only tangible and necessary goals. I do not regard war as entertainment and I shall not hesitate to use unusual tactics."

Rianlle's smile was almost openly contemptuous. "Scharrode is a small realm. Realistically, you are at the mercy of your neighbors, no matter how peculiar your campaigns."

"Your opinions of course carry great weight," said Efraim.

Rianlle went on in a measured voice. "I recall some previous discussion of a trisme, that the fortunes of Scharrode and Eccord might be joined. The subject at this moment is perhaps premature in view of the chaotic circumstances here in Scharrode."

From the corner of his eye Efraim noted a shifting of positions around the table, as tense muscles demanded relief. He met the dark gaze of Sthelany; her face seemed as pensive as ever, and—could it be true?—somehow wistful.

Rianlle once more was speaking, and everyone about the table fixed their gaze upon that unnaturally handsome face. "Nevertheless, all will no doubt sort itself out. Accommodation between our two realms must be achieved. An imbalance now exists, and I refer to the unfulfilled contract in regard to Dwan Jar, the Whispering Ridge. If a trisme will facilitate the hoped-for equilibrium, then I must give the matter serious consideration."

Efraim laughed and shook his head. "Trišme is a responsibility I do not care to assume at the moment, especially since Your Force displays such clear misgivings. Indeed, your perceptions are remarkable; you have correctly defined the situation here. Scharrode is a welter of mysteries which must be resolved before we can move onward."

Rianlle rose to his feet, as did his retinue of eiodarks. "Scharrode hospitality is as always correct, and induces us to prolong our visit, but we must take our leave. I trust that Your Force will make a realistic assessment of past, present, and putative future and act to the best interests of us all."

Efraim and Lorcas went out to the parapets of Deistary Tower and watched as Rianlle and his retinue climbed into the rented* aircar, which a moment later lifted high and flew north.

* The Rhune Realms are allowed no aircars because of their aggressive proclivities. When a Rhune wishes to make a journey he must call into Port Mar and hire a suitable vehicle for the occasion.

Lorcas had retired to his refectory to take a furtive meal; then he planned to sleep. Efraim remained on the parapets looking off over the valley, which in the light of half-aud presented so entrancing a vista that his heart missed a beat. From this land the substance of his body had been drawn; it was his own, to nurture and love and rule, for all foreseeable time; yet how useless! how forlorn! Scharrode was lost to him; he had broken the crust of tradition. Never again could he be a Rhune, nor could the damage be mended. He would never be a whole man in Scharrode, nor elsewhere; never would he be content.

He studied the landscape with the intensity of a man about to go blind. Light slanting down across Alode the Cliff illuminated a hundred forests; the irradiated foliage seemed to glow with internal light: bitter lime, intense gray-blue given pointillist fire by scarlet seed-pods, dark umber, black-blue, black-green. Surrounding stood the great peaks, each named and known in ancient fable: aloof Shanajra bearded with snow, who, resenting the mockery of the Bird Crags, turned his face to the south to stand forever brooding; the Two Hags Kamr and Dimw, rancorous above Danquil, enchanted and sleeping under a blanket of murre trees; there, Whispering Ridge, coveted by Rianlle, where the Fwai-chi walked to their sacred places among the Lenglin Mountains. His land forever, his land never; and what was he to do? In all the realm was but a single man he could trust, the Port Mar vagabond Matho Lorcas. Gosso might or might not interpret his offer as an admission of weakness. Rianlle's not too subtle threats might or might not be intended seriously. Singhalissa might yet intrigue with sufficient finesse to cause him woe. Efraim decided that he must, without further delay, call together the Scharde eiodarks, to assist him with his decisions.

The landscape dimmed, as Osmo dropped behind

Alode the Cliff. Furad hung low in the sky over Shanajra.

A slow step sounded on the marble flags; turning, Efraim saw Sthelany. She hesitated, then came to join him. Together they leaned on the parapets. From the corner of his eye Efraim studied Sthelany's face. What transpired behind that clear pale brow; what prompted the half-wistful half-mocking twist of the lips?

"Mirk is near," said Sthelany. She glanced toward Efraim. "Your Force no doubt has thoroughly reconnoitered the passages which lead here and there about the castle?"

"Only in order to protect myself from the surveillance of your mother."

Sthelany shook her head smilingly. "Is she really interested in your activities?"

"Some female of the household has demonstrated that interest. Could it be you?"

"I have never set foot in a mirk-way."

Efraim took note of the equivocation. "To answer your question precisely, I have indeed explored the mirk-ways, and I am arranging that they be interrupted by heavy iron doors."

"Then it would seem that Your Force does not intend to exercise the prerogatives of rank?"

Efraim arched his eyebrows at the question. He responded in what he hoped to be dignified tones: "I certainly do not intend to violate the persons of anyone against their will. Additionally, as I'm sure you know, the passage to your chambers is blocked by masonry."

"Indeed! Then I am reassured once and once again! It has been my habit during mirk to sleep behind triply locked doors, but Your Force's assurances make such precautions unnecessary."

Efraim wondered: did she flaunt? Did she entice? Did she tease? He said: "I might change my mind. I have adopted certain off-planet attitudes and they prompt me to confess that I find you fascinating."

"*Psssh*! These are matters we must not discuss." Sthelany, however, showed no sign of outrage.

"And what of the three bolts?"

Sthelany laughed. "I cannot imagine Your Force engaging in such an outrageous and undignified escapade; the bolts are evidently unnecessary."

Even as they spoke Furad, slipping low to the horizon, dipped half-under, and the sky went dim. Sthelany, her mouth half-open in an expression of child-like wonder, exclaimed: "Is mirk upon us? I feel a strange emotion."

Her emotion, thought Efraim, seemed real enough. Color had come to her cheeks, her bosom heaved, her eyes glowed with dark light. Furad sank even lower, all but leaving the smoky orange sky. Was mirk upon them indeed? Sthelany gasped and seemed to sway toward Efraim; he sensed her fragrance but almost as he reached to touch her hand, she pointed. "Furad floats once more; mirk is averted, and all things live!"

With no more words Sthelany moved away across the terrace. She paused to touch a white flower growing in a pot, turned a fleeting glance back over her shoulder, and then she moved on.

Efraim presently went into the castle and descended to his office. In the corridor he came upon Destian, apparently bound for the same destination. Destian however gave a frigid nod and turned aside. Efraim closed the door, telephoned the rental agency at Port Mar and ordered out an aircar, requesting a pilot other than the redoubtable Flaussig. He left the office, hesitated, turned back, locked the door and took away the key.

Chapter 9

★ ★ ★

Efraim and Matho Lorcas climbed into the aircar and were carried high above the valley of the Esch River: up, up, until they hovered on a level with the surrounding peaks. Efraim called off their names: "Horsuke, Gleide Cliff, the Tassenberg; Alode the Cliff, Haujefolge, Scarlume and Devil Dragon, Bryn the Hero; Kamr, Dimw, and Danquil; Shanajra, the Bird Crags, Gossil the Traitor—notice the avalanches—Camanche, and there: Whispering Ridge. Driver: take us yonder to Whispering Ridge."

The peaks shifted across other farther peaks of other farther realms. Under the cloud-piercing claw of Camanche, Whispering Ridge came into full view—an upland meadow rather than a true ridge, to the south overlooking Scharrode and the valley of the Esch, to the north the multiple valleys of Eccord. The aircar landed; Efraim and Lorcas jumped out into ankle-deep grass.

The air was calm. Trees grew in copses; Whispering Ridge was like an island in the sky, a place of total peace. Efraim held up his hand. "Listen!"

From an indeterminate source came a low whisper, fluctuating musically, sometimes sighing into silence, sometimes almost singing.

"Wind?" Lorcas looked at the trees. "The leaves are still. The air is still."

"Strange in itself. Up here one would expect a wind."

They moved across the sward. In the shade of the forest Efraim noticed a group of Fwai-chi watching them impassively. Lorcas and Efraim halted. "There they stand," said Lorcas, "walking their 'Path through Life,' all shags and tatters, typical pilgrims in any language."

They continued across the meadow and looked over Eccord. Belrod Strang was lost among the folds of the forested hills. "The view is superb," said Lorcas. "Do you intend to deal generously with Rianlle?"

"No. The fact remains that he could send a thousand men up tomorrow to clear the site, and another thousand to start building his pavilion, and I could do very little to stop him."

"Peculiar," said Lorcas. "Peculiar indeed."

"How so?"

"This place is magnificent—superb, in fact. I'd like a pavilion here myself. But I have been studying the maps. The realms are thick with places like this. In Eccord alone there must be twenty sites as beautiful. Rianlle is capricious to insist on this particular spot."

"Odd, I agree."

They turned back across the meadow, to find four Fwai-chi awaiting them.

As Efraim and Lorcas approached they drew a few steps back, hissing and rumbling among themselves.

The two men halted. Efraim said: "You appear disturbed. We are bothering you?"

One spoke in a guttural version of Gaean: "We walk the Life Road. It is a serious work. We do not wish to watch men. Why do you come here?"

"For no particular purpose: to look about a bit."

"I see you plan no harm. This is our place, reserved to us by a very old treaty with the kaiarks. Do you not know? I see you do not know."

Efraim gave a bitter laugh. "I know nothing—of the treaty or anything else. A Fwai drug took my memory. Is there an antidote?"

"There is no antidote. The poison breaks the roads to the memory tablets. These roads will never mend. Still, you must remind your Kaiark—"

"I am the Kaiark."

"Then you must know the treaty is real."

"The treaty won't mean much if the land is transferred to Eccord."

"That may not be done. We repeated to each other the word 'forever.' "

"I would like to see this treaty myself," sair Efraim. "I will carefully check my records."

"The treaty is not among your records," said the Fwai-chi, and the group shuffled back to the forest. Efraim and Lorcas stood looking after them.

"Now what did he mean by that?" demanded Efraim in wonder.

"He seems to feel that you won't find the treaty."

"We'll soon find out," said Efraim.

They continued across the meadow toward the aircar.

Lorcas paused and looked up toward Camanche. "I can explain the whisper. The wind pushes up over Camanche, and around. It splits and swirls and passes the meadow by. We hear innumerable small frictions: the sound of air against air."

"You may be right. Still I prefer other explanations."

"Such as?"

"The footsteps of a million dead pilgrims; cloud fairies; Camanche reckoning up the seconds."

"More convincing, I agree. Where to now?"

"Your idea of twenty equivalent sites in Eccord is interesting. I would like to look upon these sites."

They flew north, through the peaks, domes, and

ridges of Eccord; and within an hour discovered a dozen high meadows with prospects at least as appealing as those of Whispering Ridge. "Rianlle is most arbitrary," said Lorcas. "The question is, why?"

"I cannot even speculate."

"Suppose he gains the meadow and proceeds with his plans. Then what of the Fwai-chi?"

"I doubt if Rianlle would enjoy Fwai-chi pilgrims trooping through his pavilion, resting on his terraces. But how could he stop them? They are protected by the Connatic."

The aircar spiraled down into Scharrode and landed at Benbuphar Strang. As the two alighted, Efraim said: "Would you not like to return to Port Mar? I value your companionship, but there is nothing to amuse you here; I foresee only unpleasantness."

"The temptation to leave is strong," Lorcas admitted. "The food here is abominable, and I don't like to eat in a closet. Singhalissa oppresses me with her cleverness. Destian is insufferable. As for Sthelany—ah, the magic Sthelany! I hope to persuade her to Port Mar for a visit. This may seem an impossible task but every journey begins with a single step."

"So then, you plan to stay at Benbuphar Strang?"

"With your permission, still a week or two."

Efraim dismissed the aircar; the two returned to the castle. "You have exercised your charm upon her?"

Lorcas nodded. "She is curiously ambiguous. To say that she blows first hot then cold is inaccurate; she blows first cold, then colder. But she could easily order me to keep my distance."

"Has she mentioned the horrors of mirk?"

"She assures me that she bolts her doors with three bars, clamps her windows, keeps vials of offensive odors at the ready, and generally is unavailable."

They halted and looked up at the balcony behind which were Sthelany's rooms.

"A pity the mirk-way is blocked," mused Lorcas. "When all else fails one can always pounce on a girl through the dark. Still she's hinted rather pointedly that I'm not to come around. In fact, after I tried to kiss her in the Garden of Bitter Odors she told me quite bluntly to keep my distance."

"Why not try Singhalissa? Or has she also warned you off?"

"What a thought! I suggest that we take a quiet bottle of wine together and search the archives for the Fwai-chi treaty."

The Index to the Archives mentioned no treaty with the Fwai-chi. Efraim summoned Agnois, who denied all knowledge of the document. "Such an understanding, Your Force, would hardly be expressed as a formal treaty in any case."

"Perhaps not. Why does Rianlle want Whispering Ridge?"

Agnois raised his eyes to a point above Efraim's head. "I suppose that he intends to build there a summer pavilion, Force."

"Surely Rianlle treated with the Kaiark Jochaim on this matter?"

"I cannot say, Your Force."

"Who maintains the archives?"

"The Kaiark himself, with such help as he requires."

At Efraim's nod, Agnois departed.

"So now, no treaty," said Efraim glumly. "Nothing whatever to show Rianlle!"

"The Fwai-chi declared as much."

"How could they know? Our archives are nothing to them!"

"The treaty probably was an oral understanding; they knew that no document existed."

In frustration Efraim jumped to his feet. "I must take counsel; the situation has become intolerable." Once again he summoned Agnois.

"Your Force requires?"

"Send messages to the eiodarks; I wish them to meet me here in twenty hours. The occasion is urgent; I will expect everyone."

"That hour, Your Force, will fall in the middle period of mirk."

"Oh . . . in thirty hours, then. One other matter—do not inform Singhalissa of this meeting, nor Destian, nor Sthelany, nor anyone who might transfer this news; further, do not give instructions within the hearing of these people, and do not make note of the occasion upon paper. Am I sufficiently explicit?"

"Perfectly so, Your Force."

Agnois departed the room.

"If he fails me this time," said Efraim, "he'll not find me lenient." He went to the window and presently observed the departure of six under-chamberlains. "There they go with the message. The news will reach Singhalissa as soon as they return, but there is little she can do."

Lorcas said: "She's probably resigned herself to the inevitable by now. And yonder on the terrace, is that not Sthelany? With your permission, I will go out and enliven her life."

"As you like. But one word, while the thought is on my mind. The word is 'caution.' Mirk approaches. Unpleasant events occur. Lock yourself in your chambers, go to sleep, and don't stir till the light returns."

"Reasonable enough," said Lorcas slowly. "I wouldn't care to meet any gharks nor, for that matter, any hoos."

Chapter 10

★ ★ ★

After six hours of aud, Furad and Osmo left the sky. Cirse and Maddar, instead of slanting toward the horizon, settled vertically with ponderous purpose. Maddar disappeared first, to leave the land momentarily in green rowan, then Cirse sank behind Whispering Ridge. The sky flared and dimmed; darkness fell. Mirk had come to Scharrode.

In the farmsteads lights flared and flickered, then were extinguished; in the town shutters clanged, doors slammed, bolts thudded home. Those secure or fearful or uninterested in adventure took themselves to bed. Others by candlelight denuded themselves, then donned black shoulder pieces, black boots, and hideous man-masks. Others removed gray gauze gowns, to don loose smocks of white muslin; then they loosened the shutters of their windows or the bolts of their doors, but never both; then, with a small taper in one corner of the room casting almost no light at all, they lay themselves on their couches in a tremulous mixture of hope and fear, or a peculiar emotion in which perhaps one component was muted horror. Some who had bolted both shutters and door, to huddle on their couches in a ferment of arching melancholy, presently arose to unbolt door or shutter.

Through the mirk moved the grotesque shapes, taking no heed of each other. When one found the window of his choice unshuttered, he hung a white flower on the hasp, that no one else should enter; then climbing through the window he displayed himself to the silent occupant of the room—an avatar of the demon Kro.

At Benbuphar Strang, lights were extinguished, doors bolted, windows shuttered and barred as everywhere else. In the servants' quarters, some made preparations; others composed themselves to uneasy slumber. In the towers, other folk performed their own arrangements. Efraim, armed with his small pistol, bolted shutters, barred and bolted doors, searched his quarters. He checked the security of the door blocking ingress from the Sacarlatto and also that passage to the second level of Jaher Tower.

He then returned to the parlor where he threw himself into a great scarlet leather chair, poured himself a goblet of wine, and sat in gloomy meditation.

He reviewed his time on Marune and tried to assess his progress. His memory was still gone, his enemy as yet unknown. Time passed. Faces floated before his eyes. One face returned and would not depart—a pale fragile face with lustrous eyes. She had as much as assured him that her door would not be bolted. He jumped to his feet and paced back and forth. A hundred yards away she waited. Efraim stopped short and considered. No harm could come by making a trial. He need only climb to the second level of Jaher Tower, inspect the corridor; then, if all were clear, stride fifty feet to her door. Should the door be locked, he could return the way he had come. Should the door be open, Sthelany expected him.

The mask? The boots? No, they were foreign to him; he would enter Sthelany's chamber as himself.

He climbed the steps of the shortcut and came to the exit panel. He slid aside the peephole, searched the corridor. Empty.

He opened the door and listened. Silence. A faint

sound? He listened with even greater intensity. The sound might have been the blood rushing through his heart.

With stealth and care he opened the door a foot, two feet. He slipped out into the hall, feeling suddenly exposed and vulnerable. No one in sight; no sound. With racing pulse he ran to Sthelany's door. He listened. No sound. He inspected the door: six panels of heavy carved oak; three iron hinges, a heavy iron latch.

So now. He reached for the latch . . .

A sound within, a scraping as of metal. Efraim backed away and stood looking at the door. It seemed to look back at him.

Efraim moved further from the door, confused, uncertain. He retreated to the passage, closed and bolted the door, returned to his chambers.

He sank into the red leather chair and thought for five minutes. Once again he rose to his feet and, unbarring the main portal, went out into the foyer. In a storage closet he found a length of rope which he took back to his chamber, and again locked the door.

He brought out the chart of the mirk-ways and studied it for a few minutes. He then went up to the Sacarlatto, and so made his way to the unoccupied chamber directly above that of Sthelany.

He went out onto the balcony, made the rope fast, and tied a series of knots along its length, to serve as handholds and footrests. Cautiously he lowered the rope so that it hung down to Sthelany's balcony.

He descended with great care, and presently stood on the balcony. Shutters covered the glass, but a glow of light issued through a crack. Efraim pressed his eye close and peered into the room.

Sthelany sat beside a table in her usual garments. By the light of a candle she played with a toy puzzle. Beside the door stood two men in black pantaloons and man-masks. One carried a mace, the other a dagger.

Behind the door, over the back of a chair, hung a large black sack. The man with the mace pressed his ear to the door. By his posture, by the stoop of his shoulders and long powerful arms, Efraim recognized Agnois the First Chamberlain. The man with the dagger was Destian. Sthelany glanced at them, gave a slight shrug, and returned to her puzzle.

Efraim felt dizzy. He leaned on the balcony and looked off into the darkness. His stomach convulsed; he barely prevented himself from vomiting.

He did not look again into the room. With flaccid muscles he pulled himself back to the upper balcony. He hauled up the rope, coiled it, and returned to his chambers. Here he made everything secure, and placing his pistol on the table before him, poured out a goblet of wine and settled into the red leather chair.

Chapter 11

★ ★ ★

Osmo rose in the east, followed by Cirse from the south and Maddar from the southwest to dispel the dark with the gay light of isp.

Matho Lorcas was missing from his chambers; nor was he to be found anywhere within Benbuphar Strang.

The mood in the castle was taut and sullen. Agnois brought word to Efraim that Singhalissa wished an audience with him.

"She must wait until after I confer with the eiodarks," said Efraim. He could not bring himself to look at Agnois.

"I will so inform her, Your Force." Agnois' voice was gentle. "I must call to your attention a message from Kaiark Rianlle of Eccord to the members of the kaiarkal household. He invites you most urgently to a fête at Belrod Strang, during aud tomorrow."

"I will visit Belrod Strang with pleasure."

Hours of time moved past; Efraim went out into the meadow beside the castle, then wandered down beside the river. For half an hour he stood tossing stones into the water, then turned and looked back toward Benbuphar Strang—a silhouette of sinister significance.

Where was Matho Lorcas?

Efraim sauntered back to the castle. He climbed the flight of steps to the terrace and halted, reluctant to enter the oppressive dimness.

He forced himself to proceed. Sthelany, leaving the library, paused, as if wishing words with him. Efraim walked past without so much as a side-glance; in truth he dared not look at her, lest she read in his eyes the intensity of his emotion.

Sthelany stood looking after him, a forlorn and thoughtful figure.

At the time appointed, Efraim came forth from his chambers to greet the fourteen eiodarks of Scharrode, all wearing ceremonial black gowns and white vests. Their faces wore almost identical expressions of skepticism, even hostility.

Efraim ushered them into the Grand Parlor, where footmen and under-chamberlains had arranged a circular table. At the tail of the procession came Destian, dressed like the others. Efraim spoke crisply: "I do not recall summoning you to this meeting, Squire Destian, and in any event your presence will not be required."

Destian paused, glanced around the eiodarks. "What is the will of this company?"

Efraim signaled a footman: "Expel Squire Destian

instantly from the chamber, by whatever means you find necessary."

Destian managed a mocking grin, turned on his heel and departed. Efraim closed the door and joined his company. "This is an informal meeting. Feel at liberty to express yourself openly and candidly. I will respect you the more for it."

"Very good," responded one of the older eiodarks, a man solid and sturdy, brown as weathered wood. The man was Baron Haulk, as Efraim would presently learn. "I will take you at your word. Why have you expelled the Kang Destian from a colloquy of his peers?"

"There are several excellent reasons for my action, and you will learn some, if not all, of them presently. I will remind you that by protocols of rank, his title is only as good as that of his mother. As soon as I became Kaiark, she resumed her former status as the Wirwove of Urrue and Destian lapsed to Squire. A technicality perhaps, but by just such technicalities am I Kaiark and you Eiodark."

Efraim went to his place at the table. "Please be seated. I am sorry to have delayed so long with this meeting. Perhaps this apparent slight explains your lack of cordiality; am I correct?"

"Not entirely," said Baron Haulk in a dry voice.

"You have other grievances?"

"You have asked us to speak candidly. Historically those foolish enough to accept such invitations usually suffer from their boldness. Nevertheless, I will take the risk upon myself.

"Our grievances are these. First, the indifference which you show the glorious tradition of your station, and I refer to the frivolous manner in which you return to claim your place only a few days before the deadline."

"I will consider this Item One," said Efraim. "Proceed."

"Item two. Since your return you have neglected to consult the eiodarks in regard to the urgent matters which confront the realm; instead you hobnob with a person of Port Mar, whose reputation, so I have upon good authority, does him no credit.

"Item three: In a most callous manner you have insulted and inconvenienced the Kraike Singhalissa, the Lissolet Sthelany, and the Kang Destian, depriving them of status and perquisites.

"Item four. You have wilfully antagonized our ally Kaiark Rianlle of Eccord, while ignoring the bandit Gosso, who slew Kaiark Jochaim.

"Item five. As I recite these grievances, you listen with a face of bored amusement and obduracy."

Efraim could not restrain a chuckle. "I thank you for your frankness. I shall respond in the same spirit. The amused boredom and obduracy of 'Item Five' are far from my true emotions, I assure you. Before I reveal certain strange circumstances to you, may I ask whence came your information?"

"The Kang Destian has been good enough to keep us informed."

"I thought as much. Now, draw up your chairs and listen closely, and you will learn what has befallen me during these last months . . ."

Efraim spoke for an hour, withholding mention only of the events during mirk. "To summarize, I returned to Scharrode as soon as possible, but I delayed meeting the eiodarks because I wished to conceal my disability until I had in some measure repaired it. I proposed a truce to Gosso because war with Gorgetto is weary, hateful, and unproductive. Neither Gosso nor his Gorgets killed the Kaiark Jochaim; he was murdered by a Scharde traitor."

"*Murder*!" The word seemed to echo from wall to wall.

"As to Rianlle and his demands for Whispering

Ridge, I acted as any responsible Scharde Kaiark must act: I temporized until I could search the archives and discover what, if any, had been his understanding with the Kaiark Jochaim. I found no such record. In company with Matho Lorcas, I inspected Whispering Ridge. Certainly a beautiful site for a summer pavilion, but no more so than a dozen similar sites within Eccord itself. I called you here to make an exposition of the facts, and to request your best advice."

Baron Faroz said: "The question immediately arises: why does Rianlle want Whispering Ridge?"

"The single distinguishing feature to Whispering Ridge, aside from the whisper itself, seems to be the Fwai-chi regard for the place. Whispering Ridge is their sanctuary, a station along their Path of Life. The Fwai-chi claim an accord with the Kaiarks of Scharrode in regard to Whispering Ridge, though I can find no mention of this accord in the archives. So then, gentlemen, what answer shall I take the Kaiark Rianlle when I visit Belrod Strang?"

Baron Haulk said: "I doubt if we need to vote. We refuse to cede Whispering Ridge. However, put this refusal in delicate language, in order that he may save face. It is not necessary to fling the refusal in his teeth."

Baron Alifer said: "We might declare that Whispering Ridge is prone to quakes and we will not permit our friend thus to risk himself."

Baron Barwatz suggested: "The pact with the Fwai-chi must carry weight. We can show reluctance on this basis."

"I will carefully consider all your suggestions," said Efraim. "In the meantime, I must trust no one now at Benbuphar Strang. I want a complete change of staff, with the exception of Agnois. He must not be allowed to leave. Who will see to this?"

Baron Denzil said: "I will do so, Your Force."

"A second matter. My friend and confidant Matho Lorcas disappeared during mirk."

"Many persons disappear during mirk, Your Force."

"This is a special case, which I must investigate. Baron Erthe, will you be good enough to initiate a search?"

"I will do so, Your Force."

The aircar conveyed Efraim, Singhalissa, Sthelany, and Destian high over the mountains. Conversation was limited to formal exchanges. Efraim for the most part sat silently looking across the landscape. From time to time he felt Sthelany's covert gaze, and once she essayed a wan secret smile, which Efraim looked blankly past. Sthelany's charm had completely evaporated; he could hardly bear her proximity. Singhalissa and Destian discussed their cogences, a common topic during Rhune conversations. Singhalissa, among her other competences, carved cameos upon carnelians, moonstones, chalcedony, and chrysoprase; Destian collected precious minerals, and these particular cogences complemented each other.

The aircar passed above Whispering Ridge. Destian explained the geology of the region: "Essentially a great hummock of diabase broken by pegmatite dikes. A few garnets can be found in the outcrops and occasionally a tourmaline of no great value. The Fwai-chi chip them out and keep them for souvenirs, so I'm told."

"The Dwan Jar, then, lacks mineral wealth?"

"For all practical purposes."

Singhalissa turned to Efraim: "What are your thoughts regarding this bit of hillside?"

"It is a delightful site for a pavilion. The fabled whisper is discernible as a pleasant half-heard sound."

"It would seem then that you have decided to implement the agreement between the Kaiarks Jochaim and

Rianlle." Singhalissa spoke half-musingly, with the air of one reckoning imponderables.

"You state the matter too conclusively," said Efraim in a guarded voice. "Nothing is yet determined. I must verify the terms and in fact the very existence of this agreement."

Singhalissa raised her fine black eyebrows. "Surely you do not question Rianlle's word?"

"Decidedly not," said Efraim. "Still, he may have mistaken the force of the agreement. Remember, an ancient treaty with the Fwai-chi controls the region and may not honorably be ignored."

Singhalissa smiled her wintry smile. "Kaiark Rianlle might well concede the authority of this early treaty, if in fact it exists."

"We shall see. The subject probably will not arise; we have been invited to a fête, not a set of negotiations."

"We shall see."

The aircar dropped on a long slant toward Elde, Ecord's principal village. Nearby, four rivers had been diverted to create a circular waterway. At the middle of the central island stood Belrod Strang: a palace built of pale gray stone and white enameled timber, with pink, black, and silver banderoles flying from eighteen minarets. By comparison Benbuphar Strang seemed dingy and grim.

The aircar landed before the main gates; the four alighted to be met by six youthful heralds carrying gonfalons and twenty musicians pumping forth a frantic fanfare on their bruehorns.

The new arrivals were conducted to private chambers, in order that they might refresh themselves. The chambers were luxurious past the scope of Efraim's experience. He bathed in a pool of scented water, then resumed his old garments rather than put on the flaring black gown lined with flame-colored silk which had been laid out for his use. An inconspicuous door led to a water closet and a refectory, where dishes of coarse bread, cheese, cold meat, and sour beer were laid out.

Kaiark Rianlle welcomed the four in his Grand Reception Hall. On hand also were the Kraike Dervas, a tall somber woman who spoke little, and the Lissolet Maerio, reportedly Dervas' daughter by Rianlle. The relationship could easily be credited; Maerio displayed Rianlle's topaz hair and clearly modeled features. She was a person of no great stature, slight and supple, and carried herself with barely restrained animation, like an active child on its best behavior. Her amber ringlets and clear tawny skin invested her with luminosity. From time to time Efraim noticed her watching him with mournful solemnity.

Belrod Strang far exceeded Benbuphar Strang in splendor, though it fell short in that quality expressed by the Rhune term which might be translated as tragic grandeur. Kaiark Rianlle conducted himself with great affability, showing Singhalissa a conspicuous consideration which Efraim thought somewhat tactless. The Kraike Dervas behaved with formal courtesy, speaking without expression, as if reciting phrases which had become automatic to persons among whom she could not differentiate. The Lissolet Maerio by contrast seemed self-conscious and somewhat awkward. Surreptitiously she studied Efraim; from time to time their eyes met and Efraim wondered how he could ever have been attracted to Sthelany, who during mirk had worked her toy puzzle. A young black wasp was Sthelany, in company with the old black wasp who was Singhalissa.

Rianlle presently took his guests into the Scarlet Rotunda; a twenty-sided chamber with a scarlet carpet under a multicrystalline dome, fashioned like a glittering twenty-sided snowflake. A chandelier of a hundred thousand scintillas hung over a table of pink marble, the centerpiece of which was a representation of Kaiark Rianlle's projected pavilion on Whispering Ridge. Rianlle indicated the model with a gesture and a quiet smile, then disposed his guests about the table. Into the chamber came a tall man in a gray robe embroidered with black and red cusps; he pushed before him a two-wheeled cart which he stationed near Rianlle, then folded back the top to reveal trays and racks containing hundreds of vials. Maerio, sitting next to Efraim, told him: "This is Berhalten, the Master Contriver; do you know of him?"

"No."

Maerio looked right and left, lowered her voice so that Efraim alone could hear. "They say you have lost your memory; is this true?"

"Unfortunately yes."

"And that is why you disappeared from Port Mar?"

"I suppose so. I'm not certain of all the facts."

"Maerio spoke in a voice almost inaudible. "It is my fault."

Efraim was immediately interested. "How so?"

"Do you remember that we were all at Port Mar together?"

"I know this to be the case, but I don't remember."

"We spoke with an off-worlder named Lorcas. I did something he suggested. You were so stunned and shamed that your reason left you."

Efraim made a skeptical sound. "What did you do?"

"I could never tell you. I was giddy and wild; I acted on impulse."

"Did I lose my reason immediately?"

"Not immediately."

"I probably wasn't overwhelmed with horror. I doubt if you could shame me no matter how hard you tried." Efraim spoke with more fervor than he had intended. Maerio looked a bit confused.

"You must not talk like that."

"Do you find me so offensive?"

She turned him a quick side-look. "You know better than that! No. Of course not. You've forgotten all about me."

"As soon as I saw you I began to learn all over again."

Maerio whispered: "I'm afraid that you'll go mad again."

"I never went mad to begin with."

The Kaiark Rianlle spoke across the table. "I notice your admiration of the pavilion I hope to build on Whispering Ridge."

"I find the design most attractive," said Efraim. "It it interesting and well thought out, and could easily be adaped to an alternate site."

"I trust there will be no need for that?"

"I have conferred with my eiodarks. Like myself they are reluctant to cede Scharrode territory. There are difficulties in the way."

"All very well to talk of practicality," said Rianlle, still heavily jovial. "The fact remains that I have set my heart upon Whispering Ridge."

"The decision really lies beyond my discretion," said Efraim. "No matter how much I might wish to oblige you I am bound by our covenant with the Fwai-chi."

"I would like to see a copy of this covenant. Perhaps it was established for some fixed duration of time."

"I am not sure that a written version exists."

Rianlle leaned back in his chair in disbelief. "Then how can you so staunchly affirm its reality? Where have you learned its provisions? Through your own recollection?"

"The Fwai-chi have described the covenant; they are quite definite."

"The Fwai-chi are notoriously vague. On so tenuous a basis would you thwart the understanding between myself and the Kaiark Jochaim?"

"I would not wish to do so under any circumstances.

Perhaps you will supply me with a copy of this agreement that I may show my eiodarks."

Rianlle stared at him coldly. "I would find undignified the necessity to document my clear recollections."

"Your recollections are not in question," Efraim assured him. "I only wonder how the Kaiark Jochaim could bring himself to ignore the Fwai-chi covenant. I must search my archives with great diligence."

"You are unwilling to cede Whispering Ridge on a basis of trust and cooperation?"

"I certainly cannot make important decisions precipitously."

Rianlle clamped shut his mouth and swung around in his chair. "I commend to your attention the artistry of Berhalten, who has a novel concept to introduce."

Berhalten, having completed his preparations, struck a rod with his knee, to sound a reverberant gong. From the passage seven pages in scarlet and white livery ran forth. Each carried on a silver tray a small ewer. Into each of these ewers Berhalten placed a cylinder of a solid substance, layered in eight colors, whereupon the pages took up tray and ewer and set it before each person at the table. Berhalten then inclined his head to Rianlle, closed up his cart, and stood waiting.

Rianlle said, "Berhalten has discovered an amusing new principle. Notice the golden button on top of the ewer. Press this button; it releases an agent to activate the odorifer. You will be charmed . . ."

Rianlle conducted the group to a balcony overlooking a large circular stage, constructed to represent a Rhune landscape. To right and left waterfalls cascaded from stone crags, forming streams which flowed into a central pool. A chime sounded, to initiate a wild clamor of gongs and florid bruehorns, controlled by a staccato brazen tone which varied in only three degrees.* From opposite directions advanced two bands of warriors in fanciful armor, grotesque metal masks, and helmets crested with spikes and barbs. They advanced with stylistic kicks and curious bent-legged strides, then attacked and fought in ritual attitudes to the wailing clatter of martial instruments. Rianlle and Singhalissa, at one side, spoke together briefly. Efraim sat at the far end with Sthelany beside him. Destian conversed with Maerio, his exact profile tilted to advantage. The Kraike Dervas sat staring at the ballet with eyes that seemed not to follow the movement. Sthelany turned a glance toward Efraim which in those uncertain days before mirk might have caused him inner palpitations. She spoke in a soft voice: "Do you enjoy this dance?"

"The performers are very skillful. I am not a good judge of such things."

"Why are you so distant? You have hardly spoken for days."

"You must forgive me; I find the effort of ruling Scharrode no easy matter."

"When you traveled off-planet, you must have known many interesting events."

"True."

"Are the folk of the outer worlds as gluttonous and sebal as we tend to believe?"

"Their habits certainly are different from those of the Realms."

"And how did you regard these folk? Were you appalled?"

"I was in no condition to worry about anything but my own troubles."

"Ah! Cannot you answer me without evasion?"

* The Rhunes produce no true music and are incapable of thinking in musical terms. Their fanfares and clamors are controlled by mathematical progressions, and must achieve a mathematical symmetry. The exercise is intellectual rather than emotional.

"In all honesty, I fear that my casual remarks, should they be reported to your mother, might well be distorted and used to discredit me."

Sthelany sat back. For several moments she watched the ballet, which now had reached a climax with the entry of the two legendary champions Hys and Zan-Immariot.

Sthelany again turned to Efraim. "You misjudge me. I do not tell everything to Singhalissa. Do you think that I do not feel stifled at Benbuphar Strang? I yearn for new experience! Perhaps you will think ill of me for my candor, but sometimes I constrain myself to prevent outbursts of emotion. Singhalissa glorifies rigid convention; I often feel that convention must apply to others but not me. Why should folk not decorously sip wine together as they do in Port Mar? You need not look at me with such wonder; I will show you that I too can transcend convention!"

"Such occasions might well relieve the tedium. However, Singhalissa would surely disapprove."

Sthelany smiled. "Need Singhalissa know everything?"

"Very definitely not. Still she is an expert both at conducting intrigues and at sniffing them out."

"We shall see." Sthelany gave a breathless little laugh and sat back in her chair. On the stage Hys and Zan-Immariot had fought to mutual exhaustion. The lights dimmed; the instrumental tones descended in pitch and tempo, then became silent, save for a thrilling resonance of softly rubbed gongs. "Mirk!" whispered Sthelany.

Out upon the stage bounded three figures in costumes of black horn and lacquered beetle-back, wearing demon-masks.

Sthelany leaned closer to Efraim. "The three avatars of Kro: Maiesse, Goun, and Sciaffrod. Notice how the champions strive! Ah! they are slain. The demons dance in triumph!" Sthelany turned toward Efraim; her shoulder touched his. "How it must be on the one-sun worlds where day and mirk alternate!"

Efraim glanced sidewise. Sthelany's face was close; her eyes shone in the stage glow. Efraim said: "Your mother looks this way. Peculiar! She seems neither surprised nor annoyed that we talk in an intimate manner."

Sthelany stiffened and leaning forward watched the demons stamping the corpses of the dead heroes into the dust, throwing their heads low, tossing them high, plunging arms low, thrusting them high.

Later, as the four guests took their leave, Efraim had a moment to pay his respects to Maerio. She said, somewhat wistfully, "I did not appreciate that you had become friendly with Sthelany. She is most fascinating."

Efraim managed a painful grin. "Appearances can be deceiving. Can you, will you, be discreet?"

"Of course."

"I believe that Singhalissa instructed Sthelany to pretend intimacy, to beguile me into a foolish act whereby she might discredit me with the Scharde eiodarks. In fact—"

Maerio asked breathlessly, "In fact, what?"

Efraim found that he could not express himself both with precision and delicacy. "I will tell you some other time. But it is you, not Sthelany, whom I find fascinating."

Maerio's eyes suddenly glistened. "Good-by, Efraim."

As Efraim turned away he surprised Sthelany's gaze upon him, and it seemed that he saw there a hurt, wild, desperate expression. This was the same face, Efraim reminded himself, that had indifferently considered the workings of a toy puzzle while two men with mace, dagger, and sack waited by the door.

Efraim went to make his formal farewell to the Kaiark Rianlle. "Your hospitality is on a most magnificent scale. We could not think to duplicate it at Benbuphar Strang. Still, I am hoping that before long you will return our visit, in company with the Kraike and the Lissolet."

Rianlle's face showed no geniality. He said: "I accept the invitation, for myself and for the Kraike and Lissolet as well. Will you think me presumptuous if I set the occasion for three days hence? You will have had opportunity to search for the legendary covenant, and also to consult your eiodarks and to convince them that the accord between Kaiark Jochaim and myself must without fail be implemented."

Words pressed against Efraim's lips; he contained them with an effort.

"I will consult my eiodarks," he said at last. "We will reach a decision which may or may not please you, but which will be based upon how we regard our duty. In any event we shall look forward to entertaining you at Benbuphar Strang at the time you suggest."

Chapter 12

★ ★ ★

On their return to Benbuphar Strang the portals were thrown wide by footmen strange to Efraim.

Singhalissa stopped short. "Who are these people? Where is our old staff?"

"I have replaced them," said Efraim. "All except Agnois, whom you will still find in office."

Singhalissa turned him a curious glance. "Must all our arrangements be disrupted? Why have you done this?"

Efraim spoke in his most formal voice. "I wish to live among people who have no prior loyalties and on whom I can place reliance. I took steps to achieve this by the only possible means: a complete change."

"My life daily grows more hectic," cried Singhalissa. "I wonder where this turmoil will end! Do you also plan to take us to war for a miserable fragment of hillside?"

"I would like to know why Rianlle is so exercised over this 'miserable fragment of hillside.' Do you know?"

"I am not in the Kaiark Rianlle's confidence."

A footman approached. "Your Force, the Baron Erthe is at hand."

"Please introduce him."

The Baron Erthe came forward. He looked from Efraim to Singhalissa and back to Efraim. "Your Force, I have a report to render."

"Speak."

"In a rubbish heap near Howar Forest we discovered a corpse in a black sack. It has been identified as the remains of Matho Lorcas."

Efraim's stomach quivered. He looked at Singhalissa, who showed no emotion. But for a soft metallic scrape behind the door he would have been the corpse in the black sack, rather than Matho Lorcas.

"Bring the corpse to the terrace."

"Very well, Your Force."

Singhalissa said softly, "Why do you do that?"

"Can't you guess?"

Singhalissa turned slowly away. Efraim summoned Agnois. "Place a trestle or a bench on the terrace."

Agnois allowed an expression of puzzlement to cross his features. "At once, Your Force."

Four men carried a coffin across the terrace, and set it down upon the trestle. Efraim took a breath and lifted the lid. For a moment he looked down into the dead face, then he turned to Agnois. "Bring the mace."

"Yes Force." Agnois started away, then halted and stared back aghast. "Which mace, Force? There are a dozen on the wall of the trophy room."

"The mace with which the Noble Lorcas was murdered."

Agnois turned and walked slowly into the castle. Efraim, gritting his teeth, examined the corpse. The head was crushed, and a wound in the back gave evidence of a dagger thrust.

"Close the lid," said Efraim. "There is no more to be learned. Where is Agnois? He loiters, he tarries!" He signaled a footman. "Find Agnoís, ask him to make haste."

The footman presently returned on the run. "Agnois is dead, Force. He has taken poison."

Efraim clapped him on the back. "Return inside; make inquiries! Discover the circumstances!"

He turned sadly back to Baron Erthe. "One of the murderers has escaped me. Be so good as to bury this poor corpse."

In due course the footman reported his findings. Agnois, upon entering the castle, apparently had gone directly to his quarters and there swallowed a fatal draught.

Efraim bathed himself with unwonted zeal. He took a dismal meal in his refectory, then lay down on his couch. For six hours he dozed, tossed, twisted, dreamed evil dreams, then slept soundly from sheer exhaustion.

Efraim had not yet dismissed the aircar which had

transported him to Belrod Strang. He now ordered the pilot to convey him to Whispering Ridge.

The aircar rose into the light of the colored suns and flew north around the flank of Camanche, then drifted down to settle on the grass. Efraim alighted, and walked out across the meadow. The serenity was that of lost Arcadia; except for the crag to the east, the view was of clouds and air; isolation from the anxieties, plots, and tragedies of Benbuphar Strang was complete.

At the center of the meadow he paused. The whisper was not perceptible. A moment passed. He heard a sigh, a mingling of a million soft tones, each no louder than a breath. The sigh became a murmur, faded tremulously, rose again, then dwindled toward silence—a sound of elemental melancholy . . . Efraim heaved a deep sigh of his own and turned toward the forest, to find, as before, a group of Fwai-chi watching from the shade. They shambled forward; he advanced to meet them.

"Before mirk I came here," said Efraim. "Perhaps I spoke to one of you?"

"We were all here."

"I am faced with problems, and they are your problems as well. The Kaiark of Eccord wants Whispering Ridge. He wants to build a pavilion here for his pleasure."

"That is not our problem. It is yours. The men of Scharrode have promised to defend our holy place forever."

"So you say. Do you possess a document attesting to this agreement?"

"We have no document. The promise was exchanged with the kaiarks of old and transferred to each successive kaiark."

"Kaiark Jochaim may so have informed me, but your

drugs took my memory, and now I can assert nothing of my own knowledge."

"Still, you must enforce the covenant." The Fwai-chi returned into the forest.

Efraim despondently returned to Benbuphar Strang. He called a meeting of the eiodarks and reported Rianlle's demands. Certain of the eiodarks cried out for mobilization; others sat glum and silent.

"Rianlle is unpredictable," declared Efraim. "At least this is my opinion. Our preparation for war might dissuade him. On the other hand, he would not care to retreat before our defiance, when our resources are inferior to his. Perhaps he will send his troops to occupy the Dwan Jar and then ignore our protests."

"We should occupy the Dwan Jar first, and fortify it!" cried Baron Hectre. "Then we might ignore the protests of Rianlle!"

Baron Haulk said: "The concept is attractive, but the terrain hinders us. He can bring his troops around Camanche and up Duwail Slope; we can supply our forces only by the trail across the front of Lor Cliff, and Rianlle alone on the brink could interdict us. We would more profitably fortify Bazon Scape and the pass at the head of the Gryphon's Claw, but there we invade Eccord soil and prompt sure retaliation."

"Let us look at the physiograph," said Efraim.

The group filed into the octagonal Hall of Strategies. For an hour they studied the thirty-foot-long scale model of Scharrode and the adjoining lands, but only verified what they already knew: if Rianlle sent troops to occupy the Dwan Jar, then these troops would be vulnerable to attack along their supply routes and might well be marooned. "Rianlle may not be able to exercise his strength as effectively as he hopes," mused Baron Erthe. "We may force him into a stalemate."

"You are optimistic," said Baron Dasheil. "He can marshal three thousand sails. If he brings them here"—he pointed to a scarp overlooking the valley—"he can drop them down into Scharrode while our troops are occupied along Bazon Scape. We can either harass his position on the Dwan Jar, or we can guard the vale against his sails. I cannot define a system whereby we can do both."

Efraim asked: "How many sails can we ourselves muster?"

"We have fourteen hundred eagles and as many winglets."

"Perhaps we could send twenty-eight hundred sails against Belrod Strang."

"Suicide. The glide is too long; the air sweeps down the Groaning Crags."

The group returned to their places around the red syenite table.

Efraim said: "As I understand it, no one feels that we can effectively resist Eccord, if Rianlle decides to wage war in earnest. Am I right?"

No one contradicted him.

Efraim went on. "One point we have not discussed is why Rianlle is so anxious to obtain Dwan Jar. I cannot credit the pavilion theory. I have just returned from Whispering Ridge. The beauty and isolation are too poignant to be borne; I could think only of human transience and the vanity of hope. Rianlle is proud and stubborn, but is he insensitive? I find his plans for a pavilion farfetched."

"Agreed, Rianlle is proud and stubborn," said Baron Szantho, "but this fails to explain his initial commitment to the project."

"There is nothing else on the Dwan Jar but the Fwai-chi sanctuary," Efraim remarked. "What profit could he gain from the Fwai-chi?"

The eiodarks considered the matter. Baron Alifer said tentatively: "I have heard a rumor that Rianlle's splendors exceed his income, that Eccord cannot support his fantasies. I could not discredit any theory that he hopes to exploit a hitherto untouched resource—the Fwai-chi. To guard their sanctuary they would be forced to pay him a toll of drugs, crystals, elixirs."

Baron Haulk said: "None of this bears upon our own problems. We must decide upon a policy."

Efraim looked around the table. "We have examined all our options except one: submission to Rianlle's demands. Does the council believe this to be our only feasible course of action, detestable though it is?"

"Realistically, we have no other choice," muttered Baron Haulk.

Baron Hectre pounded his fist on the table. "Can we not assume a defensive posture, even though it is only bluff? Rianlle may think better of forcing the issue!"

Efraim said: "Let us adjourn until next aud, and at that time we will reach a decision."

Again Efraim met with his eiodarks. There was little conversation; all sat with glum faces. Efraim said, "I have searched the archives. I find no sure reference to an agreement with the Fwai-chi. They must be betrayed, and we must submit. Who disagrees?"

"I disagree," growled Baron Hectre. "I am willing to fight."

"I am willing to fight," said Baron Faroz, "but I do not care to destroy myself and my folk to no purpose. We must submit."

"We must submit," said Baron Haulk.

Efraim said, "If the Kaiark Jochaim indeed acceded to Rianlle's demands, he must have been subjected to these same pressures. I hope that our humiliation serves a good purpose." He rose to his feet. "Rianlle arrives here tomorrow. I hope that all of you will be on hand, to lend the occasion dignity."

"We will be here."

Chapter 13

★ ★ ★

An hour before arrival of the Kaiark Rianlle, the eiodarks gathered on the terrace of Benbuphar Strang. Through psychological processes perhaps differing from case to case many attitudes had hardened, and where, before, shameful misgivings had been converted into defiance. Where before all the eiodarks had resigned themselves to submission, now it seemed as if all had been inspired to obduracy.

"Rianlle challenged your memory?" cried out Baron Balthazar. "With reason, you admit. He cannot challenge mine. If the Fwai-chi declare the existence of this covenant and if the archives at least hint of its existence, then I distinctly recall the Kaiark Jochaim discussing this same covenant."

"I as well!" declared Baron Hectre. "He dare not challenge us."

Efraim laughed sadly. "He will dare; why not? You are powerless to damage him."

"This shall be our strategy," said Baron Balthazar. "We will deny his demands with fortitude. If he invests the Dwan Jar with his troops, we shall harass them and destroy his work. If Rianlle wafts his sails down into our vale, we shall plunge down from Alode Cliff and rip their wings."

Baron Simic shook his fists into the air. "It shall not be so easy for Rianlle after all!"

"Very well," said Efraim. "If this is how you feel, I

am with you. Remember, we shall be firm but not pugnacious; we shall mention self-defense only if he threatens. I am glad that, like myself, you find submission intolerable. And there, I believe, around Shanajra, comes Rianlle and his party."

The aircar landed; Rianlle alighted, followed by the Kraike Dervas, the Lissolet Maerio, and four Eccord eiodarks. The heralds quickstepped forth, producing ceremonial fanfares. Rianlle and his party marched to the steps leading up to the terrace; Efraim and the Scharde eiodarks descended to greet them.

Formalities were exchanged, then Rianlle, throwing back his handsome head, stated: "Today the Kaiarks of Scharrode and Eccord meet to certify an era of warm regard between their realms. It pleases me, therefore, to state that I will look favorably upon the possibility of trisme between yourself and the Lissolet Maerio."

Efraim bowed his head. "This is a most gracious offer, Force, and nothing could accord more to my own inclinations. But you are fatigued from the journey; I must allow you to refresh yourself. In two hours we shall meet in the Grand Parlor."

"Excellent. I may assume that you have found no further objections to my little scheme?"

"You may be sure, Your Force, that good relations between our two realms, on the basis of equity and cooperation, are the foundation of Scharde policy."

Rianlle's face darkened. "Can you not respond to the point? Do you or do you not intend to cede the Dwan Jar?"

"Your Force, let us not transact our important business upon the front steps. When you have rested an hour or two, I will clarify the Scharde point of view."

Rianlle bowed, swung about. Under-chamberlains

conducted him and members of his party to the chambers which had been prepared for them.

Maerio stood by a tall arched window looking out across the valley. She rubbed her hand on the stone sill, thrilling at the coarse contact. How would it be to live here at Benbuphar Strang, among these tall shadowy chambers, surrounded by echoes? Many strange events had occurred here, some of which made dreary listening; nowhere in all the Realms, so it was said, could be found a castle so riddled with mirkways. Efraím had changed; as to this there was no denying. He seemed more mature, and he seemed to obey the Rhune conventions tentatively, without conviction. Perhaps this was all to the good. Her mother, Dervas, had once been as gay and as artless as herself, but Rianlle (whom she supposed to be her father) had insisted that the Kraike of Eccord must exemplify the Rhune Code, and Dervas was impelled to orthodoxy for the good of the realm. Maerio wondered about Efraim. He hardly seemed the sort to insist on orthodoxy. In fact, from her own experience she knew better!"

A slight sound behind her; she whirled about. A panel in the wainscoting had slid aside and there stood Efraim.

He crossed the room and stood smiling down into her face. "Forgive me for startling you. I wanted to see you secretly and alone, and I knew no other way."

Maerio looked toward the door. "Let me shoot the bolt; we must not be discovered."

"True." Efraim bolted the door and returned to Maerio. "I have been thinking of you; I cannot get you out of my mind."

"I have been thinking of you too, especially since I learned that the Kaiark planned to join us in trisme."

"That is what I must tell you. As much as I long for

such a trisme, it will never occur, because the eiodarks intend to fight rather than give up the Dwan Jar."

Maerio nodded slowly. "I knew this would happen . . . I don't want to go in trisme anywhere else. What shall I do?"

"For now nothing. I can only make plans for war."

"You might be killed!"

"I hope not. Give me time to think. Would you run away with me, away from the Realms?"

Maerio asked breathlessly, "Where would we go?"

"I don't know. We would not be privileged as we are now; we might be forced to toil."

"I will go with you."

Efraim took her hands. She shivered and closed her eyes. "Efraim, please! You will lose your memory again."

"I don't think so." He kissed her forehead. She gasped and drew back.

"I feel so strange! Everyone will recognize my agitation!"

"I must go now. When you have composed yourself, come down to the Grand Parlor."

Efraim returned through the mirk-way to his chambers, and arrayed himself in formal garments.

A knock at the door. Efraim looked at the clock. Rianlle so soon?

He opened the door to find Becharab, the new First Chamberlain. "Yes, Becharab?"

"Your Force, before the castle stand several natives. They wish to speak with Your Force. I told them you are resting, but they are insistent."

Efraim ran past Becharab, across the reception hall and foyer, to the haughty astonishment of Singhalissa who stood conversing with one of the eiodarks from Eccord.

Before the terrace stood four Fwai-chi—ancient brown-red bucks, all tatters and shags. A pair of footmen, making fastidious faces, attempted to shoo them away. The Fwai-chi, discouraged, were starting to sidle off when Efraim appeared.

He ran down the steps, motioned the footmen aside. "I am Kaiark Efraim. You wished to see me?"

"Yes," said one, and Efraim thought to recognize the old buck he had met up on Whispering Ridge. "You claim that you remember no covenant in regard to the Dwan Jar."

"That is true. The Kaiark of Eccord who wants the Dwan Jar is here now."

"He must not have it; he is a man who demands much. If he were to control the Dwan Jar, he would demand more, and we would be forced to glut his avarice." The Fwai-chi produced a dusty vial containing half a gill of dark liquid. "Your memory is locked and there are no keys to the locks. Drink this liquid."

Efraim took the vial and examined it curiously. "What will it do to me?"

"Your corporeal substance itself contains memory; it is called instinct. I give you a medicine. It will prompt all your cells to erupt memories—even those very cells which now block your memory. We cannot unlock the doors; but we can batter them open. Do you dare take this draught?"

"Will it kill me?"

"No."

"Will it make me insane?"

"Perhaps not."

"Will I know everything I knew before?"

"Yes. And when you have your memory, you must protect your sanctuary."

Efraim went thoughtfully up the steps.

By the balustrade Singhalissa and Destian stood waiting. Singhalissa asked sharply: "What is that vial?"

"It contains my memory. I need only drink it."

Singhalissa leaned forward, her hands quivered.

Efraim moved back. She asked: "And will you drink it?"

"Naturally."

Singhalissa chewed at her lip. Efraim's vision suddenly seemed totally keen and clear; he noticed the lack of bloom on Singhalissa's skin, the minute wrinkles around her eyes and mouth, the bird-like thrust of her sternum.

"This may seem an odd point of view," said Singhalissa, "but consider. Events go well for you! You are Kaiark; you are about to make trisme with a powerful realm. What else do you need? The contents of the vial may well disturb these conditions!"

Destian spoke with an air of authority: "If I were in your position, I would let well enough alone!"

Singhalissa said: "You have best confer with Kaiark Rianlle; he is a wise man; he will advise you."

"The matter would seem only to concern myself," remarked Efraim. "I doubt if Rianlle's wisdom can apply in this case." He passed into the reception hall, to meet Rianlle coming down the grand staircase. Efraim paused. "I hope you enjoyed your rest."

Rianlle bowed politely. "Very much indeed."

Singhalissa came forward. "I have urged Efraim to solicit your advice in a very important matter. The Fwai-chi have provided him a liquid which they claim will restore his memory."

Rianlle reflected. "Excuse me a moment or two." He took Singhalissa aside; the two conversed in mutters. Rianlle nodded and thoughtfully returned to where Efraim waited.

"While I rested," said Rianlle, "I reviewed the situation which has caused a tension between our realms. I propose that we postpone further consideration of Dwan Jar. Why allow so paltry a matter to interfere with the trisme I have suggested? Am I not correct?"

"Entirely."

"However, I have no confidence in Fwai-chi drugs. Often they promote cerebral lesions. In view of our prospective relationship I must insist that you do not dose yourself with some vile Fwai-chi potion."

Very odd, thought Efraim. If the truncation of his memory were so advantageous to other folk, then the disadvantage to himself would seem correspondingly great. "Let us join the others who await us in the parlor."

Efraim seated himself at the red table and looked around the faces: fourteen Scharde and four Eccord eiodarks; Singhalissa, Destian, Sthelany; Rianlle, the Kraike Dervas, Maerio, and himself. He carefully placed the vial on the table before him.

"There is a new circumstance to be considered," said Efraim. "My memory. It is contained in this bottle. At Port Mar someone robbed me of my memory. I am intensely anxious to learn the identity of this person. Of the folk who were with me in Port Mar, two are dead—by coincidence, or perhaps not coincidentally after all, both were murdered.

"I have been advised not to drink this draught. I am told that it is best to let sleeping dogs lie. Needless to say, I reject this point of view. I want my memory back, no matter what the cost." He unstoppered the vial, raised it to his mouth and poured the contents down his throat. The flavor was soft and earthy, like pounded bark and mold mixed with stump water.

He looked around the circle of faces. "You must forgive this act of ingestion before your very eyes . . . I feel nothing yet. I would expect a delay while the material permeates my blood, courses around my body . . . I notice a shifting of lights and shadows—your faces flicker. I must shut my eyes . . . I see splashes of light: they shatter and burst . . . I see everywhere in my body . . . I see with my hands and inside my legs and down my back." Efraim's voice became hoarse.

"The sounds—everywhere . . ." He could speak no more; he leaned back in his chair. He felt, he saw, he heard: a jumble of impressions: whirling suns and dancing stars, the froth of salt spume, the warmth of swamp mud, the dank flavor of waterweeds. The thrust of spears, the scorch of fire, and screaming women. Timelessness: visions swarmed past, then back, then away, like shoals of fish. Efraim became faint; his legs and arms went numb. He fought away the lethargy, and watched in fascination as the first furious explosion of images retreated and swirled away. The succession of sensations continued, but at a pace less blurred, as if to the control of chronology. He began to see faces and hear voices: strange faces, strange voices, of persons inexpressibly dear, and tears ran down his cheeks. He felt the extent of space; he knew the grief of departures, the exultation on conquest; he killed, he was killed; he loved and knew love; he nurtured a thousand families; he knew a thousand deaths, a thousand infancies.

More slowly came the images, as if the source were almost drained. He was the first man to arrive on Marune; he led the tribes east from Port Mar; he was all the Kaiarks of Scharrode and of many other realms as well; he was many of the ordinary folk; he lived all these lives in the course of five seconds.

Time began to decelerate. He watched the construction of Benbuphar Strang; he prowled by mirk; he scaled the Tassenberg and struck a blond warrior toppling down the face of the Khism. He began to see faces to which he could almost put names; he was a tall auburn-haired child who grew into a tall spare man with a bony face and short thick beard. With beating heart Efraim followed this man whose name was Jochaim through the chambers of Benbuphar Strang, by aud, isp, umber, and rowan. By mirk he wandered the mirk-ways, and he felt the intoxication of striding forth, clad only in shoulder-piece, man-mask, and boots into the chamber of his sometimes terrified elect. To Benbuphar Strang came the maiden Alferica from Cloudscape Castle, to be taken in trisme by Jochaim, and in due course a child was born who was named Efraim, and Jochaim faded from consciousness.

Efraim's youth passed. His mother, Alferica, drowned during a visit to Eccord; presently to Benbuphar Strang came a new Kraike, Singhalissa, with her two children. One of these was dark vicious Destian; the other, a pale big-eyed waif, was Sthelany.

Tutors educated the three children; they chose cogences and eruditions. Sthelany professed the writing of poetry in an abstruse poetic language, the working of mothwing tapestry, and star-names, as well as the contriving of fumes and fragrances which all well-born ladies were expected to include among their skills. She also collected Glanzeln flower vases, glazed an ineffable transparent violet, and unicorn horns. Destian collected precious crystals, and replicas of medallions on the hilts of famous swords; he also professed heraldry and the intricate lore of fanfares. Efraim professed the architecture of castles, mineral identification, and the theory of alloys, although Singhalissa considered the choice insufficiently erudite.

Efraim politely acknowledged Singhalissa's remarks and put them to the back of his mind. He was First Kang of the Realm; Singhalissa's opinions need not concern him.

Singhalissa herself professed a dozen skills, didactics, and expertises; she was quite the most erudite person of Efraim's acquaintance. Perhap once a year she visited Port Mar, that she might buy supplies and materials for the specialized needs of those at Benbuphar Strang. When Efraim learned that Kaiark Rianlle of Eccord, with the Kraike Dervas and the Lissolet Maerio, planned to accompany Jochaim and Singhalissa to Port Mar, he decided to join the party. After considerable discussion, Destian and Sthelany also decided to undertake the journey.

Efraim had been acquainted with Maerio for years, under the formal circumstances imposed upon all visits between kaiarkal households. At first he considered her frivolous and eccentric. She lacked all erudition, she was clumsy with the vials, and she seemed always to be restraining herself from some reckless spontaneity, which caused Singhalissa's eyebrows to twitch and Sthelany to look away in ostensible boredom. These very factors induced Efraim to cultivate Maerio. Gradually he noticed that her company was extraordinarily stimulating, and that she was remarkably pleasant to look at. Forbidden thoughts wandered into his mind; he ejected them from loyalty to Maerio, who would be shocked and horrified!

The Kaiark Rianlle, Kraike Dervas, and Maerio flew over the mountains to Benbuphar Strang; on the morrow all would journey to Port Mar. Rianlle, Jochaim, Efraim, and Destian gathered in the Grand Parlor for an informal talk; bobbing their heads behind etiquette screens they discreetly took small cups of arrack.

Rianlle was at his best. Always a remarkable speaker, on this occasion his conversation was brilliant. Like Singhalissa, Rianlle was most erudite; he knew the Fwai-chi signals and all the trails of their "Path through Life"; he knew the Pantechnic Metaphysic; he had collected and studied the insects of Eccord, and had indited three monographs upon the subject. Additionally Rianlle was a notable warrior, with remarkable exploits to his credit. Efraim listened to him with fascination. Rianlle was discussing Dwan Jar, the Whispering Ridge. "It has occurred to me," he told Jochaim, "that here is a site of sublime beauty. One of us should make use of it. Be generous, Jochaim; let me build myself a summer garden with a pavilion on the

Dwan Jar. Think how I would rest and muse to the wild whispering sound!"

Jochaim had smiled. "Impossible! Have you no sense of fitness? My eiodarks would drive me forth for a madman if I agreed to your proposal. Additionally, I am bound by a covenant with the Fwai-chi. Certainly you are making a joke."

"No joke whatever. Truly I covet that bit, that trifle, that insignificant wisp of land!"

Jochaim shook his head. "When I am dead, I can no longer oppose; Efraim must then assume that responsibility. While I live, I must deny you your fancy."

Rianlle said: "It would seem that by the process of dying, you withdraw your opposition. I would not have you dead on that account, however. Let us talk along easier subjects . . ."

The group had flown into Port Mar, and as usual taken accommodation at the Royal Rhune Hotel, where the management knew and respected their customs . . .

Efraim raised his head from his hands and looked wildly around the table. Taut faces everywhere; eyes fixed upon him; silence. He closed his eyes. Recollections came soft and slow now, but with a wonderful luminous clarity. He felt himself leaving the hotel in company with Destian, Sthelany, and Maerio for a stroll through Port Mar, and perhaps a visit to the Fairy Gardens, where Galligade's Puppets provided entertainment.

They walked down the Street of Brass Boxes and across the bridge into New Town. For a few minutes they strolled along the Estrada, peering into the beer gardens where the folk of Port Mar and students from the college drank beer and devoured food in full view of everyone.

Efraim at last asked direction from a young man emerging from a book shop. Seeing the party to be

Rhunes, he volunteered serving as their escort to the Fairy Gardens. To everyone's disappointment the entertainment was at an end. Their guide introduced himself as Matho Lorcas and insisted upon ordering a bottle of wine, along with suitable etiquette screens. Sthelany raised her eyebrows in a fashion reminiscent of Singhalissa and turned away. Efraim, catching Maerio's eye, sipped the wine, protected by the propriety of the screen. Maerio, greatly daring, did likewise.

Matho Lorcas seemed a person of buoyant disposition and irrepressible wit; he refused to allow either Sthelany or Destian to sulk. "And how are you enjoying your visit?" he asked.

"Very much," said Maerio. "But surely there is more excitement than this? We always think of Port Mar as a place of wild abandon."

"Not quite accurate. Of course this is the respectable part of town. Doesn't it seem so to you?"

"Our customs are rather different," said Destian frostily.

"So I understand, but here you are in Port Mar; why not attempt the Port Mar customs?"

"That logic does not quite follow," murmured Sthelany.

Lorcas laughed. "Of course not! I wondered if you'd agree. Still—don't you have any inclination to live—well, let us say, normal lives?"

Efraim asked: "You think we don't live normal lives?"

"Not from my point of view. You're smothered in convention. You're walking bundles of neuroses."

"Peculiar," said Maerio, "I feel quite well."

"I feel well," said Efraim. "You must be mistaken."

"Aha! Well, possibly. I'd like to visit one of the Realms and see how things go for myself. Do you like the wine? Perhaps you'd prefer punch."

Destian looked around the table. "I think we'd better return to the hotel. Haven't we seen enough of New Town?"

"Go, if you like," said Efraim. "I'm in no hurry."

"I'll wait with Efraim," said Maerio.

Matho Lorcas spoke to Sthelany. "I hope you'll wait too. Will you not?"

"Why?"

"I want to explain something which I believe you want to hear."

Sthelany languidly rose to her feet and without a word moved off. Destian, with a dubious look back at Efraim and Maerio, followed.

"A pity," said Lorcas. "I found her extremely attractive."

"Sthelany and Destian are both most stately," said Maerio.

Lorcas asked with a sly smile, "And what of you? Aren't you stately too?"

"When ceremony makes demands on me. Sometimes I find Rhune ways rather tiresome. If Efraim weren't here I'd try that punch. I'm not ashamed of my inner workings."

Efraim laughed. "Very well. If you will, I will too. But wait until Destian and Sthelany are out of sight."

Matho Lorcas ordered rum punch for all. Efraim and Maerio drank first behind the screens, then spluttering with embarrassed laughter, brought the goblets into the open and drank.

"Bravo!" declared Lorcas soberly. "You have taken a long step on the road to emancipation."

"It doesn't amount to all that much," said Efraim. "I'll buy another round. Lorcas, what about you?"

"With pleasure. Still, it wouldn't do for the two of you to stagger into the hotel drunk, would it?"

Maerio clasped her head. "My father would turn purple. Of all the folk alive he is the most rigid."

"My father would simply look the other way," said

Efraim. "He seems rigid, and of course he is, but essentially he is quite reasonable."

"So, you two are not related?"

"Not at all."

"But you're fond of each other?"

Efraim and Maerio looked sidewise at each other. Efraim laughed uncomfortably. "I won't deny it." He looked again at Maerio, whose face was twisting. "Have I offended you?"

"No."

"Then why do you look so doleful?"

"Because we must come to Port Mar to tell each other such things."

"I suppose it is absurd," said Efraim. "But Port Mar is so much different from Eccord and Scharrode. Here I can touch you, and it is not mirk." He took her hand.

Matho Lorcas heaved a sigh. "Ah me. I should leave you two alone. Excuse me a moment; for a fact there is someone I wish to see."

Efraim and Maerio sat together. She leaned her head against his shoulder; he bent down, kissed her forehead. "Efraim! It is not even mirk!"

"Are you angry?"

"No."

Lorcas appeared beside the table. "Your friend Destian is here."

Efraim and Maerio drew apart. Destian approached and looked curiously from one to the other. He addressed Maerio. "The Kaiark Rianlle has asked me to conduct you back to the hotel."

Efraim stared up at Destian, who, so he knew, was not above misrepresenting facts. Maerio, sensing friction, jumped to her feet. "Yes. I'll welcome some rest, and look! with umber and the overcast and the shade from these enormous trees it is almost like mirk!"

Destian and Maerio departed. With a debonair gesture Lorcas settled into the seat beside Efraim. "And that is the way things go, my friend."

"I am embarrassed," said Efraim. "What will she think of me?"

"Get her alone somewhere and find out."

"That is impossible! Here in Port Mar perhaps we lost our equilibrium. In our realms we could never consider such display." He rested his chin on his hands and looked gloomily across the restaurant.

"Come along," said Lorcas. "Let's move down the avenue. I'm due at the Three Lanterns presently; first I'll show you a bit of the town."

Lorcas took Efraim to a cabaret frequented by students. They listened to music, drank light beer. Efraim explained to Lorcas how life went in the Realms. "A place like this by comparison seems a zoo of fecund animals. The Kraike Singhalissa, at least, would adopt this view."

"And you respect her judgment?"

"To the contrary; this is the principal reason I am here. I hope to discover benefits and redemptions in what I confess seems sickening behavior. Look at that couple yonder. Sweating, panting, shameless as dogs in rut. At the very least their activity is unhygienic."

"They are relaxed. Still, yonder other folk sit quite decorously, and none seem offended by the antics of the two reprobates."

"I am confused," admitted Efraim. "Trillions inhabit Alastor Cluster; not all can be deluded. Perhaps anything and everything is innocent."

"What you see here is relatively innocent," said Lorcas. "Come, I'll show you places less so. Unless you prefer your illusions, so to speak?"

"No. I will come with you, as long as I do not have to breathe too much fetid air."

"When you've seen enough, just say the word." He

glanced at his watch. "I have just an hour to spare, then I must go to work at the Three Lanterns."

The two walked up the Street of Limping Children, then turned along the Avenue of Haune, Lorcas pointing out the more disreputable places of the town—an expensive bordello, bars frequented by sexual deviates, and a dim establishment, purportedly a tea shop which operated illegal nerve machines in the upper rooms; other sordid places offering even more questionable entertainment.

Efraim observed all with a stony face. He found himself not so much shocked as detached, as if what he saw were intended as a grotesque stage-setting. At last they reached the Three Lanterns, a rambling old structure from which issued the sound of fiddles with banjos playing merry jigs after the style of the Tinsdale Wayfarers.

Singhalissa was right, thought Efraim, when she declared music no more than symbolic sebalism—well, perhaps "sebalism" was not quite the right word. "Passion," perhaps, which encompassed sebalism and all the other strong emotions as well. At the Three Lanterns, Lorcas took his leave of Efraim. "Remember, I'd be enchanted for the opportunity to visit the Realms. Perhaps someday—who knows?"

Efraim, thinking of the frigid reception Lorcas would certainly receive at the hands of Singhalissa, restrained an invitation. "Perhaps some day. At the moment it might not be convenient."

"Good-by then. Remember, directly back down the Avenue of Haune, turn south on any of the side streets to the Estrada, and along to the bridge. Then up the Street of Brass Boxes to your hotel."

"I am exactly oriented; I will not get lost."

Somewhat reluctantly Lorcas went into the Three Lanterns; at the entrance he waved farewell. Efraim turned back the way they had come.

Clouds hung heavy; the time was yet umber, though very dull. Furad hung low behind Jibberee Hill, and both Maddar and Cirse were obscured by overcast. Gloom almost as dense as mirk shrouded Port Mar, and colored lights invested the Avenue of Haune with a tipsy gaiety.

As Efraim walked, his thoughts returned to Maerio; how he wished she were with him now! But futile to counter the will of the Kaiark Rianlle, whose rectitude was matched only by that of Singhalissa.

Efraim at this moment was passing the expensive bordello, and even as he reflected upon the character of the Kaiark Rianlle, out the door of the bordello, his face blurred and clothes disheveled, stepped the Kaiark Rianlle himself.

Efraim stared, unbelievingly. He began to laugh first incredulously, then with the intoxication of total mirth.

Rianlle stood with his mouth first open, then closed; first swelling with purple wrath, then trying to achieve a comradely grin. Under the circumstances neither could be convincing or effective. Ridicule to a Rhune was insupportable; when Efraim told the story, as surely he must—the episode was too good to keep; even Rianlle realized this—the Kaiark Rianlle would thereafter be a figure of fun, and furtive snickers would accompany him through life.

Rianlle by dint of some desperate inner contortion composed himself. "What are you doing out along the avenue?"

"Nothing! Investigating weird antics!" And Efraim again began to chuckle. Rianlle managed a steely grin. "Ah, well, you must not judge me too harshly. Unfortunately for myself, I am expected to represent the apotheosis of Rhune gallantry. The pressure becomes overwhelming. Come along; we will take a hot drink together as the folk do without shame here at Port

Mar. The drink is called coffee and is not considered intoxicating."

Rianlle led the way along the Street of the Clever Flea to an establishment called "The Great Alastor Coffee Emporium." He ordered the refreshment for both, then excused himself. "A moment; I have a small errand."

Efraim watched Rianlle cross the avenue and enter a dingy little shop whose windows were crowded with all manner of goods.

The coffee was served; Efraim tasted the brew and found it savory, aromatic, and to his liking. Rianlle returned; the two sipped coffee in cautious silence.

Rianlle lifted the lid to the silver ewer in which the coffee was served, peered within. His hand hovered a moment over the open mouth of the ewer, then the lid dropped with a clang. He poured a second cup for Efraim and a second cup for himself. He now became affable and expansive. Efraim drank more coffee, although Rianlle allowed his own portion to go cold. And Efraim's mind dimmed and lost itself in floating mists.

As if in a dream he felt himself walking with Rianlle along the Estrada, across the bridge, and by back alleys into the park at the Royal Rhune Hotel. Rianlle approached the hotel with great stealth; but as luck would have it, the path curved and Singhalissa stood before them.

She looked in disgust from Efraim to Rianlle. "You have found him in a state of intoxication! What shame! Jochaim will be furious!"

Rianlle considered a moment, then shook his head despondently. "Come with me, away from the path, and I will explain how things have gone."

On a secluded bench Rianlle and Singhalissa sat; Efraim stood watching a firefly. Rianlle cleared his throat. "Affairs are more serious than simple intoxication. Someone offered him a dangerous drug which he foolishly ingested; his memory has completely been destroyed."

"What a tragedy!" cried Singhalissa. "I must inform Jochaim; he will turn New Town topsy-turvy, and never stop until he learns the truth!"

"Wait!" said Rianlle in a low hoarse voice. "This may not be to our best interests."

Singhalissa fixed Rianlle with a cool stare which seemed to see everything. "*Our* best interests?"

"Yes. Consider. Jochaim must ultimately die—perhaps sooner than we might wish. When that unhappy event occurs, Efraim will become Kaiark."

"In his present condition?"

"Of course not. He will rapidly become whole and alert, and Jochaim will renew his memories. But—what if Efraim goes traveling?"

"And does not return?"

"On Jochaim's death, Destian than becomes Kaiark of Scharrode, and I will give him Maerio in trisme. Jochaim will never surrender Whispering Ridge; if I hold it I can levy a great toll upon the Fwai-chi. What, after all, are gems and elixirs to them? If Destian is Kaiark there will be no difficulty."

Singhalissa reflected. "Do not underrate Destian; he is obstinate at times! But he would never deny me, were I Kraike of Eccord. In all candor, Belrod Strang is more to my taste than gloomy old Benbuphar."

Rianlle grimaced and uttered a soft involuntary moan. "What of Dervas?"

"You must dissolve the trisme; this is simple enough. If events proceed along these lines all will go well. If not, it is best that we forget the matter and I will take Efraim in to Jochaim. Never fear! Jochaim is both pertinacious and ruthless; he is fond of Efraim and will never stop until he learns all the circumstances!"

Rianlle sighed. "Destian shall be next Kaiark of

Scharrode. We will then celebrate two trismes: between Destian and Maerio; between you and me."

"In that case, we will work together."

Though Efraim overheard much of their conversation, the subject matter made little impression on him.

Singhalissa went off, to return with a shabby gray suit and scissors. She cut Efraim's hair short, and the two dressed him in the gray suit. Then Rianlle, stepping into his rooms, emerged wearing a black cape and a helmet which concealed his face.

Efraim's recollections blurred. He barely recalled walking to the spaceport, nor embarcation aboard the *Berenicia*, where money changed hands between Rianlle and the steward.

Events gradually merged into his conscious recollections. He opened his eyes to look into the face of the Kaiark Rianlle. Once again he saw that mixture of rage, shame, and desperate affability Efraim had noted on the Avenue of Haune.

"My memory is whole," said Efraim. "I know the name of my enemy and I know his reasons. Cogent reasons, they are. But these are personal matters and I will deal with them on a personal basis. Meanwhile other more important affairs compel our attention.

"With the return of my memory I can now assert that the Kaiark Jochaim did indeed endorse the ancient covenant with the Fwai-chi, and that, also, he made to the Kaiark Rianlle the following remark: 'Only when I am dead will I abandon my opposition to your scheme,' which the Kaiark Rianlle interpreted as 'when I am dead, there shall be no further opposition to your scheme.' A most reasonable mistake, which the Kaiark Rianlle now appreciates. I suspect that he wishes to withdraw utterly and forever his claim to the Dwan Jar; am I right, Your Force?"

"Quite correct," stated the Kaiark Rianlle in a monotone. "I see where I misinterpreted the Kaiark Jochaim's jocularity."

"Three more matters should be considered," said Efraim. "Your Force, I apply to you for trisme between our houses and our realms."

"I am honored to accede to your proposal, if the Lissolet Maerio is like-minded."

"I agree," said Maerio.

"Temporarily I will abandon this happy subject," said Efraim, "to deal with the crime of murder."

"Murder!" The dreadful word rustled around the table.

"The Kaiark Jochaim," continued Efraim, "was murdered by a bolt in the back. The bolt was not discharged by a Gorget bore, hence the murderer is Scharde. Better to say, he accompanied the Scharde force.

"Another murder occurred during mirk. I am in a sense too close to this crime to avoid prejudice; hence you, the eiodarks of Scharrode, shall hear my evidence; you shall pass judgment, and I will not quarrel with your findings.

"I speak now as a witness.

"When I arrived at Benbuphar Strang in company with my friend Matho Lorcas, I encountered the coolest of welcomes, and in fact antagonism.

"A few days before mirk the Noble Sthelany surprised me by her cordiality and her assurances that for the first time she planned not to bolt her doors during mirk." Efraim described the events previous to, during, and after mirk.

"It is clear that an attempt was made to entice me into Sthelany's chambers; but poor Lorcas entered in my stead, or else he was recognized and murdered to prevent him from telling me of the trap.

"I well understand that strange deeds are done during mirk, but this murder falls into a different category.

It was planned a week or more before mirk, and put into execution with cruel efficiency. It is not a mirk-deed. It is murder."

"The assertions are malicious fabrications," said Singhalissa. "They are too feeble to deserve refutal."

Efraim turned to Destian. "What is your comment?"

"I can only echo the Noble Singhalissa's remarks."

"And Sthelany?"

Silence. Then presently a low voice: "I will say nothing, except that I am sick of life."

At this point, in embarrassment, the party from Eccord departed from the Grand Parlor. The eiodarks went off to the far end of the room. For ten minutes they muttered together, then returned.

"The judgment is this," said Baron Haulk. "The three equally share guilt. They are guilty not of mirk-deed, but murder. They shall this moment be shaved bald and expelled from the Rhune Realms, carrying no property except the clothes on their backs. Forever they are exiled and no Rhune Realm will take them in. Murderers, at this moment divest yourselves of all jewels, ornaments, and valuables. Then go down to the kitchens where your heads will be shaved. You will then be escorted to the aircar and flown to Port Mar, where you must live as best you can."

Chapter 14

★ ★ ★

Maerio and Efraim stood on the parapets of Benbuphar Strang. "Suddenly," said Efraim, "we are at peace. Our difficulties have dissipated. Life lies before us."

"I fear that new difficulties are just beginning."

Efraim looked at her in surprise. "How can you say so?"

"It is clear you have known life outside the Realms; I have had the merest hint of a taste. Will we be content to live as Rhunes?"

"We can live in whatever fashion suits us," said Efraim. "I want nothing but happiness for both of us."

"Perhaps we will want to travel to far worlds. What then? How will the Schardes regard us on our return? They will consider us tainted—not true Rhunes."

Efraim looked away down the valley. "We are not Rhunes of the clearest water, for a fact. So then—what shall we do?"

"I don't know."

"I don't know either."

Attention:

DAW COLLECTORS

Many readers of DAW Books have written requesting information on early titles and book numbers to assist in the collection of DAW editions since the first of our titles appeared in April 1972.

We have prepared a several-pages-long list of all DAW titles, giving their sequence numbers, original and current order numbers, and ISBN numbers. And of course the authors and book titles, as well as reissues.

If you think that this list will be of help, you may have a copy by writing to the address below and enclosing fifty cents in stamps or coins to cover the handling and postage costs.

DC SUPER HERO ADVENTURES

SUPERMAN™ AND THE BIG BOUNTY

WRITTEN BY
MICHAEL ANTHONY STEELE

ILLUSTRATED BY
LEONEL CASTELLANI

SUPERMAN CREATED BY
JERRY SIEGEL AND JOE SHUSTER
BY SPECIAL ARRANGEMENT WITH THE JERRY SIEGEL FAMILY

STONE ARCH BOOKS
a capstone imprint

Published by Stone Arch Books, an imprint of Capstone.
1710 Roe Crest Drive
North Mankato, Minnesota 56003
www.capstonepub.com

Library of Congress Cataloging-in-Publication Data
Names: Steele, Michael Anthony, author. | Castellani, Leonel, illustrator.
Title: Superman and the big bounty / by Michael Anthony Steele ; illustrated by Leonel Castellani.
Description: North Mankato, Minnesota : Stone Arch Books, an imprint of Capstone, [2021] | Series: DC super hero adventures | "Superman created by Jerry Siegel and Joe Shuster by special arrangement with the Jerry Siegel Family." | Audience: Ages 8-11. | Audience: Grades 4-6. | Summary: Racing through the solar system, the Man of Steel tries to rescue a captive of Lobo the bounty hunter.
Identifiers: LCCN 2020027220 (print) | LCCN 2020027221 (ebook) | ISBN 9781515882169 (library binding) | ISBN 9781515883258 (paperback) | ISBN 9781515892311 (pdf)
Subjects: CYAC: Superheroes—Fiction. | Supervillains—Fiction. | Bounty hunters—Fiction.
Classification: LCC PZ7.S8147 Su 2021 (print) | LCC PZ7.S8147 (ebook) | DDC [Fic]—dc23
LC record available at https://lccn.loc.gov/2020027220
LC ebook record available at https://lccn.loc.gov/2020027221

Designer: Hilary Wacholz

Printed in the U

TABLE OF CONTENTS

Years ago in a distant galaxy, the planet Krypton exploded. Its only survivor was a baby named Kal-El who escaped in a rocket ship. After landing on Earth, he was adopted by the Kents, a kind couple who named him Clark. The boy soon discovered he had extraordinary abilities fueled by the yellow sun of Earth. He chose to use these powers to help others, and so he became the guardian of his new home.

He is . . .

SUPERMAN™

A Call for Help

Danny Wilkes was already running late for work. Wearing his sharply pressed suit, he dodged traffic as he crossed the busy street. Once at his car, he fumbled through his pocket for his keys. He carefully balanced the cardboard tray of coffee cups he carried as he quickly unlocked his door. Danny sighed with relief as he slid into the driver's seat and shut the door behind him. He might not be late after all.

The car door swung back open.

"What in the world?" Danny asked as he closed the door again. It swung open again—all by itself.

As Danny reached for the door handle, the car seat bucked beneath him. "Hey!" he shouted as it tossed him out of the car.

THUNK! SPLOOSH!

Danny landed on the hard pavement under a shower of hot coffee.

"Hey!" repeated someone nearby.

"My word!" said another.

"What's going on?" asked someone else.

Danny's eyes widened as he watched other drivers being hurled from their cars all down the street.

KRASH! KRUNCH! KRASH! KRASH!

One by one, cars lurched forward, smashing into the vehicles in front of them. People scrambled to get clear as their cars created a long, single-file crash. Glass shattered and metal creaked as the vehicles fused together somehow. Then the entire creation rose off the street as if it were alive.

Danny joined the screaming crowd as they ran for safety. It looked as if he wasn't the only one who was going to be late this morning.

* * *

On the other side of Metropolis, Lois Lane stood beside Clark Kent's desk at the *Daily Planet* newspaper office. The reporter was flipping through her notebook as she ran through the last of her notes. She wanted to see if her recent investigation had any ties to Clark's latest news story.

"Well, what do you think, Clark?" Lois frowned when she realized her fellow reporter was no longer listening.

"Hello?" Lois asked. She waved a hand in front of his face. "Earth to Clark."

Clark had only missed her last few sentences. Thanks to his super-hearing, his attention had been on something else—the cries of alarm and sounds of destruction coming from across town.

He shook his head. "I'm sorry, Lois." He sprang to his feet. "I just remembered . . . I have to meet with a source for a new story."

Lois crossed her arms and smirked. "Been holding out on me, Smallville?" She often used Clark's hometown as a nickname.

"Not really." Clark smiled. "This is brand new . . . *really* new."

Clark ducked into the nearby stairwell and sped up the steps. He removed his glasses and loosened his tie as he neared the roof. Clark hadn't actually lied to Lois. From the combination of sounds he had heard, a big news story probably was waiting for him across the city. And, as Superman, he was going right to the source.

WHOOSH!

The roof's door flew open, and a blue and red streak rocketed out. Superman circled the shining globe atop the building before flying toward the emergency. Blurry skyscrapers whizzed by as he sped over the city.

As Superman neared the scene, he spotted plumes of smoke rising up from the destruction. He also saw the long tail of some enormous creature. It disappeared around a building as he approached.

What is that? Superman thought.

The Man of Steel raced after the creature. He darted around the corner as the tail was about to disappear behind yet another building.

"Oh, no you don't," Superman said as he grabbed onto the tail. He dug his heels into the pavement, keeping the creature from escaping.

That's when he noticed the long tail was actually made of metal. More than that, it was formed from a bunch of cars fused together.

As Superman held tight, the end of the tail snapped off in his arms. He dropped the piece and scanned the crushed cars with his X-ray vision. Luckily, no one was trapped inside. That's when the strangest thing happened.

KRACK! KREEEEEK! KRUNCH!

The broken piece suddenly reattached itself. The metal creaked and groaned as it joined with the rest of the tail.

"It's time to see what kind of creature this belongs to," he said as he rose off the ground.

Superman didn't have to find the other end of the metallic creature; it came to him. Before he could move, the head of a giant snake appeared around the corner. Its long body of connected cars gathered beneath it as it rose into the air. It looked ready to strike.

Superman balled up his fists, preparing to attack. Unfortunately, the metal snake struck first. With lightning speed, it wrapped him tightly in its coils. Superman struggled to break free as the metal snake brought him closer to its gaping mouth.

Just when he expected to be swallowed whole, Superman instead saw a small creature inside the snake's mouth. He had glowing eyes, green skin, and four arms. He was so small that he was strapped inside a child's car seat.

"Hello, Superman," the creature said, waving two of its hands. "I'm sorry about the mess. But I had to get your attention somehow."

The coils loosened, and Superman flew free. "Do I know you?"

"My name is Xal Gliknark, from the planet Balvin," the alien said as he unbuckled himself and hopped to the ground. "But most people just call me the Mechanic." He gestured back to the snake. "Because I can control just about any kind of machinery."

"Why did you need my attention?" Superman asked.

"Actually, I need your help!" the tiny alien corrected. The Mechanic nervously rubbed his four hands together. "I'm being hunted, across the galaxy, by the most vile, disgusting creature who ever . . ."

VROOOOOOOOOM!

A deep, rolling rumble suddenly filled the air. The sound grew louder as a noisy hoverbike came into view. It swooped down from the sky, leaving a trail of black smoke behind it.

The alien driving the vehicle was dressed in leather and had a chain and hook wrapped around one arm. His chalk-white skin glistened in the sun, and his thick, black hair ruffled in the wind. He pulled to a stop in front of them.

The Man of Steel groaned at the sight of this particular alien. It was Lobo—an intergalactic bounty hunter and general pain in the neck, as far as Superman was concerned.

"Hi-ya, Supes," Lobo said in a deep, gravelly voice. He hopped off the hoverbike and spread his arms wide. "Long time, no see, pal!"

Mechanical Trouble

Superman frowned at the new arrival. "I thought I told you never to return to Earth, Lobo."

"What? You were serious about that?" the bounty hunter asked, eyes wide as if with surprise. He gently placed a hand to his chest. "I'm hurt! Well, don't you worry, I'll just collect my bounty and let you get back to whatever weird super hero business you have going here."

The Mechanic took a couple steps back and hid behind Superman's cape.

"I'm afraid I can't let you do that," the hero said. "The Mechanic is now under my protection."

Lobo moved closer to Superman. "Now you see there . . . *that's* gonna be a problem." The bounty hunter pointed down at the Mechanic. "Because some nice folks are paying me mucho credits to bring this guy in." He jutted a thumb at his own chest. "And I don't have to tell you, the Main Man always delivers."

"Listen, Lobo—" Superman began.

POW! With lightning speed, Lobo lurched forward and punched the Man of Steel. The Mechanic barely jumped clear as Superman flew across the street and slammed into a nearby building.

The hero shook his head as he climbed out of a crater in the side of the marble wall. He had forgotten just how hard Lobo could hit. The bounty hunter was as strong and invincible as he was.

WHOOSH!

Superman pushed off the building and flew toward Lobo. The Man of Steel put Lobo in a bear hug before flying straight up. He carried the bounty hunter high into the clouds.

"Come on, Supes," Lobo said with a chuckle. "Quit playing around."

Lobo puffed out his chest and flexed his arm muscles, breaking Superman's grip. Then he balled his hands together and swung them at the hero with all his might. Superman soared through the clouds while Lobo dropped like a stone.

The bounty hunter whistled loudly and his hoverbike flew up to meet him. Lobo plopped onto the seat and revved the engine.

VROOOM! VROOOM!

He aimed the bike toward the Mechanic. "All right, little guy," Lobo growled. "Now that your bodyguard is gone, let's go for a ride."

Lobo sped toward the tiny alien. As he neared, he reached out and prepared to snatch the little guy off the ground. To the bounty hunter's surprise, he was the one grabbed—plucked right off his bike.

"Hey!" Lobo shouted as he tried to wriggle free. He turned to see that the giant car snake held him by the scruff of his leather jacket. He looked down at the alien. The Mechanic's eyes glowed as he glared back up at the bounty hunter.

"Are you doing that?" Lobo asked. "That's a neat trick." The bounty hunter snarled. "I hate neat tricks!"

BAM!

Lobo punched a hole in the head of the car snake, but it didn't release him. Instead, it wrapped the bounty hunter in its massive coils. Metal creaked and Lobo grunted as it squeezed him tighter. "No . . . giant snake is going . . . to crush . . . the Main Man!"

WHOOOSH!

Suddenly, the Mechanic was swooped off the ground.

"Let's get you out of here," Superman said as he flew the alien out of harm's way. "And far away from the city, so no one will get hurt. Maybe then I can talk some sense into Lobo."

"I don't think that's possible," said the Mechanic.

The Man of Steel flew out of the city and across the harbor. Jets of water trailed behind them as they zoomed just above the ocean's surface.

BZZZZZ!

Superman picked up a buzzing sound with his super-hearing. He glanced back just in time to see a missile speeding toward them. The hero banked to one side in the nick of time.

THOOM!

The missile exploded, and the two tumbled toward the sea. The Man of Steel straightened out and flew toward a nearby oil derrick. He set the alien on the deck among many confused crew members.

"Wait here," the hero told him. "I'll take care of Lobo."

"But I can help," said the Mechanic.

Superman smiled at him. "You came to me for help, remember?" He leaped into the sky and zipped toward Lobo.

The bounty hunter fired another missile, but this time, Superman was ready. His eyes narrowed and two thin, red beams shot from them. The beams from his heat vision went straight for the missile.

Ka-THOOM!

Superman flew through the explosion and raced toward the bounty hunter.

Lobo laughed. "Come to Papa!" he yelled before leaping off his hoverbike. He slammed into the super hero and laid into him like a punching bag.

"Let's . . . talk about this," Superman said, between punches.

"Nothing to talk about, Big Blue," Lobo replied. "The little guy is my bounty, and I'm here to collect."

HELP! HELP!

Shouts of alarm caught Superman's attention. Below them, the crew members on the oil derrick leaped into the ocean as the structure came to life. Part of the huge structure walked forward like a giant spider.

What is the Mechanic doing? Superman thought. *Someone's going to get hurt.*

He dropped Lobo and flew to help. He swooped down and grabbed a lifeboat in each hand. He dropped them near the floating crew members and began helping them aboard.

Meanwhile, Lobo dropped onto his hoverbike and hit the gas. The bike roared as he went for the Mechanic.

The bounty hunter laughed as he flew toward the derrick. The spiderlike creature swung at him with long crane arms and drill pipes. The bounty hunter gripped the handlebars of his hoverbike tighter and dodged every attack.

"I've taken on Anderian thorn spiders bigger than this," Lobo said with a laugh. "This is nothing!" He loosened the chain and hook from around his arm.

WHOOP-WHOOP-WHOOP-WHOOP!

Lobo swung the chain over his head as he approached the Mechanic. The little alien's eyes glowed brighter as he controlled the derrick's movements. He made the rig shoot a jet of oil at the approaching bounty hunter.

Lobo dipped his bike and easily flew under the black stream. Then he zipped close and wrapped the chain around the Mechanic's body. He snatched him out of the mechanical spider and flew up to the clouds.

With the alien gone, the oil derrick returned to normal. As Superman placed two crew members into a lifeboat, he saw Lobo and the Mechanic getting away.

Superman sighed. "Dealing with Lobo can never be simple."

CHAPTER 3

No Holding Back

Earth shrank behind them as Lobo and the Mechanic rocketed through space. The bounty hunter gripped the handlebars of his hoverbike while the short alien rode on the seat behind him. The Mechanic was wrapped up in Lobo's chain, to keep him in place.

"I don't understand why you are doing this!" the Mechanic said. "Where are you taking me?"

Lobo let out a deep laugh. "You'll find out soon enough."

VROOM! VROOM!

The bounty hunter revved the throttle, increasing their speed. Within seconds they shot past the Moon.

"And if you don't give me any more trouble, I'll let you stay awake for the ride." Lobo turned and grinned at him. "Because if I see one more monster snake or giant spider-thing, it's a bop on the head and lights out for you."

As Lobo faced front once more, the Mechanic's eyes began to glow. Suddenly, the bounty hunter's hoverbike jerked to the left, then to the right.

"Hey!" Lobo shouted, trying to regain control of his vehicle. "What's going on?!"

The bike flew up into a somersault and then spun in a corkscrew. Lobo fought with the handlebars, trying to stay on the bike. He became furious when he realized it was the Mechanic's doing.

"Messing with the Main Man's ride?" Lobo asked. "That's just not right!"

"Take me back to Earth," the Mechanic demanded.

GRRR! Lobo growled through gritted teeth. "Not . . . happening." He gripped the handlebars tighter.

"Very well," said the little alien. "You asked for it."

The hoverbike dipped and sped through space. It soon approached the nearest planet, which loomed large before them like a huge, crimson ball.

Lobo tried to hit the brakes as the red planet grew closer. But it was no use. They fell faster and faster. The hoverbike punched through the thin atmosphere and raced toward a red desert.

Lobo was able to pull up at the last second before they slammed into the ground. The bounty hunter and his bounty were thrown from the bike amid a giant plume of red sand.

* * *

Superman flew the last oil-rig worker to the lifeboat.

"Thanks, Superman," the crew member said. "Who was that scary guy on the bike?"

The Man of Steel looked up at the sky and let out a sigh. "Someone who thinks he's getting away."

FWOOSH!

Wind rocked the lifeboats as Superman shot up into the clouds. He left Earth's atmosphere and hovered in space. He squinted and glanced around, looking for any sign of the bounty hunter.

"Lobo's bike polluted the sky," Superman said. "Maybe it left a trail out here too."

Using his superpowered vision, the hero quickly spotted a thin trail of pollution snaking off into space. Superman's lips tightened as he took off after the bounty hunter.

The thin trail led all the way to Mars. As he flew closer, Superman scanned the planet's surface for any sign of the bounty hunter. He quickly located a crash site. A long trench stretched across the sand.

Superman spotted Lobo at the end of that trench. The bounty hunter sat on the ground next to a toolbox as he made repairs to his bike. An unconscious Mechanic was tied to the back of it.

Superman lightly touched down next to the scene.

"Hi-ya, Supes," Lobo said without looking up. "Hand me that wrench there, will ya?"

Superman ignored the request and moved toward the Mechanic. The small alien was out cold. The hero scanned him with his X-ray vision but could find no broken bones.

"Gee, thanks for nothing," Lobo said under his breath. He grabbed the wrench himself. "I thought you were supposed to help people."

"Is he all right?" Superman asked.

"Who? Sleeping Beauty over there?" Lobo asked as he put the finishing touches on his bike. "That genius knocked himself out . . . with a crash *he* caused, mind you."

Superman crouched beside the alien. "I'm taking him back to Earth."

Lobo threw the wrench back in the toolbox and stood. "There you go again," he said. "Always with the crazy ideas."

Superman spread his arms wide. "Look around you, Lobo. This is an empty planet. There aren't any innocent bystanders to distract me." He balled his fists. "And I don't have to hold back."

"Yeah, I know." Lobo chuckled as he marched closer. "Sounds like fun," he said just before head-butting the Man of Steel.

WHAM!

The powerful blow drove Superman into the ground like a nail. Only his head and shoulders poked out of the red sand.

Lobo leaned over him. “Now, what were you saying?”

POW!

Superman’s fist erupted from the sand, and the bounty hunter was knocked backward. The Man of Steel burst from the ground and flew up to meet Lobo. Not holding back in the least, the hero belted the bounty hunter as hard as he could. Lobo snarled as he was propelled away, disappearing over the horizon.

Superman knew he couldn’t hurt Lobo, but maybe that last punch would buy him enough time to get the Mechanic. He flew back toward the hoverbike. Unfortunately, his super-hearing picked up Lobo’s whistle.

VROOM! VROOM! Before Superman could grab the alien off the bike, the vehicle revved to life and zoomed away.

Superman flew after it as it raced through deep canyons and over steep mountains. The Man of Steel pushed harder, closing in on the bike. He was almost on top of it, reaching out to grab the Mechanic as they flew beneath a thick stone arch.

"Hey, Supes!" yelled Lobo. "Catch!"

Superman glanced up to see the bounty hunter standing atop the arch. He hurled down a boulder the size of a school building. The hero let the bike pull away as he reached up to catch the enormous rock. Superman grunted as he held it aloft long enough for the hoverbike to get clear. Then the boulder slammed to the ground, pinning the hero beneath it.

Lobo laughed as he leaped off the arch and landed next to an even bigger boulder, one the size of a small stadium. The bounty hunter growled as he lifted the huge rock above his head. He carried it a few steps before slamming it onto the first rock. Superman was pinned beneath tons of Martian rock.

Lobo dusted off his hands as his hoverbike pulled up next to him. "And that's why you don't mess with the Main Man!"

He hopped on and revved the engine. Black smoke belched from his tailpipes as he flew away from the planet and into space.

CHAPTER 4

A Fleet of Problems

BOOM!

Superman punched through the last of the boulders and climbed out. Lobo and the Mechanic were nowhere to be found.

"I don't care if he drops a mountain on me," Superman said as he dusted off his uniform. "He is *not* getting away."

The super hero took to the skies, more determined than ever to stop Lobo.

The bounty hunter had been correct about one thing. Superman was supposed to help others. The Mechanic had come all the way to Earth for help. So far, the Man of Steel had let him down. Lobo was just as strong as Superman and couldn't be hurt. So brute force wasn't going to stop him. And so far, Lobo couldn't be reasoned with either.

There has to be some other way to handle this bounty hunter, Superman thought.

The hero followed Lobo's trail away from the planet and out of the solar system. Stars streaked by as Superman hurried to catch up with him.

Luckily, the hero finally found Lobo at a standstill. The bounty hunter sat on his hoverbike surrounded by two different fleets of spaceships. The Mechanic was still out cold on the seat behind him.

"For the last time," Lobo said, "move aside or I start annihilating!"

"We don't take orders from Juran spies," came a voice from the communicator on Lobo's bike.

"Don't be ridiculous! He's not our spy!" said another voice. "He is obviously a Talescian spy. Note the dull features, clear evidence of low intelligence."

Lobo covered his face with both hands. "That's it! I'm blasting everybody!"

Superman raced in front of Lobo and held out his arms. "I think we can all solve this peacefully."

"Oh, hey, Supes," Lobo said with a nod. He pointed to the fleets. "Can you believe these guys? They want to involve the Main Man in their stupid little war."

Superman rounded on the bounty hunter. "Listen, Lobo. You can't solve all your problems with senseless violence."

FUUUUUSH!

A missile shot from beneath Lobo's hoverbike.

"Sorry, Supes. I wasn't listening," Lobo said with a grin. "I was too busy solving my problem with senseless violence."

Superman sighed and squinted at the missile. Two thin, red beams shot from his eyes and struck the projectile. It exploded harmlessly before reaching the fleet.

"To all Juran ships," shouted a voice from Lobo's communicator. "Half of you fire at the Talescians, the other half at the intruders."

"Prepare to return fire!" ordered the Talescian commander.

Guns from both fleets aimed at each other as well as at Superman and Lobo.

Superman turned to the fleets. "Wait, please!"

Lobo rubbed his hands together. "Now things are about to get interesting."

Superman didn't know what he was going to do. How could he stop everyone, including Lobo, from attacking one another?

Luckily, he didn't have to.

A small, green sphere appeared around him. Two larger ones formed around each of the space fleets. Even Lobo and the unconscious Mechanic floated in their own green spheres. Superman smiled. He recognized those balls of green light.

"Am I interrupting something?" asked a familiar voice. "I hope I am."

"Lantern Jordan!" shouted the Juran commander. "We didn't know you were nearby."

The Green Lantern, Hal Jordan, floated closer. His power ring glowed as he kept the green spheres in place.

"I'm glad you are," Superman said with a smile. "Good to see you, Hal."

"What are you doing out here, Superman?" Green Lantern asked before glancing at Lobo. "Oh . . . I get it."

Superman nodded at the fleets. "You know these people?"

Hal nodded and sighed. "Yeah, the planets Juray and Talesca are in my space sector," he explained. "As a member of the Green Lantern Corps, I helped them work out a peace treaty a few years ago."

"Which we were following," said the Juran commander. "Until these Talescian spies showed up."

"They're your spies!" the Talescian commander shot back.

"All right, all right," Green Lantern said. "I assure you that none of these people are spies."

"Yeah! The Main Man is not a spy," Lobo agreed. Then he shrugged. "Unless the money's good."

"Please keep to the treaty and return to your planets," Green Lantern continued. "Thank you." He released the ships from their green spheres.

Just then, the guns on all the ships came to life. They swung about and pointed in one direction. All of them were aimed at Lobo.

"We have lost control of the guns!" the Talescian shouted. "This is not our doing!"

Superman had an idea who was behind it. He turned to see that the Mechanic was now wide-awake. His eyes glowed as he floated inside his own protective sphere.

VOOM! TZAP! TZAP! VOOM! VOOM!

Lasers and missiles exploded from every ship. Hal Jordan created a green shield to block the lasers. Meanwhile, Superman flew out and punched every missile he didn't stop with his heat vision.

Lobo hopped on his hoverbike, revved the engine, and flew toward the nearest ship. He loosened his chain and swung it over his head.

"Oh, yeah!" the bounty hunter shouted. "Time for some first-class destruction!"

"Lobo!" Superman shouted. "Don't hurt anyone!"

The bounty hunter shook his head. "You're no fun at all." He brought his chain around, merely smashing the guns poking out of the ships.

TZAP! POW! POW! Ka-THOOM!

For a brief moment, Superman, Green Lantern, and Lobo worked together to fend off the attacks. Explosions of every color washed out the stars around them.

I have to convince the Mechanic to stop controlling the ships, Superman thought.

Unfortunately, Lobo beat him to it. While the two heroes were occupied, the bounty hunter drove his hoverbike toward the small alien and punched through the sphere surrounding him.

Superman watched as Lobo pulled a small canister from his belt and flipped a switch. Gas filled the sphere, knocking out the little alien. Lobo threw him over his shoulder and took off.

VROOM!

Once again, Lobo sped away with his bounty.

The Main Man Delivers

With the Mechanic gone, the spaceships stopped firing. Soon after, Green Lantern and Superman destroyed the last of the roving missiles.

"Let me get this straight," Green Lantern said, giving a small wave to the spaceships as they headed back to their home planets. "Are you saying you chased Lobo all the way out here from Earth?"

“That’s right,” Superman said. The hero explained how the Mechanic came to him for help. “But the trouble is, that bounty hunter and I are so evenly matched. I can barely slow him down.”

“I’m sure you’ll think of something,” Hal told him. He held up his ring. “I come across many challenges, but I can’t solve them all with my power ring. Sometimes I have to think of more creative solutions.”

“You’re probably right,” Superman replied. “But I have to catch up to him first.”

Hal smiled. “My power ring can help with that.” He extended his arm and green light shot from his ring. The light formed into a sleek, one-man spaceship. “This should last long enough for you to find him.”

“Thanks,” Superman said as he climbed into the ship.

The cockpit hatch closed and Superman gripped the controls. Then the hero was slammed back in his seat as the ship rocketed through space.

Superman concentrated as he steered the craft, still following the hoverbike's trail. Stars streamed past as he moved through space faster than he ever had before. He couldn't help but smile at the thrill of going so swiftly, even for him.

The ship slowed as a huge space station came into view. The base was enormous, but it looked as if it was falling apart. Large structures seemed to barely be attached, while other pieces simply floated beside it.

Nevertheless, Superman spotted Lobo pulling up to it on his hoverbike. The bounty hunter climbed off his bike and floated through an air lock on the side of the station.

I hope I'm not too late, Superman thought.

As he raced closer, the green spaceship around him flickered out of existence. Now he simply flew toward the base and through the air lock.

HSSSSSS!

The door opened and Superman stepped into the corridor. Lobo walked a few feet ahead of him. The unconscious Mechanic was still draped like a sack of potatoes over his shoulder.

"Hold it right there, Lobo," Superman ordered. "This is as far as you go."

Lobo spun around. He dropped the alien and grinned.

"Oh, yeah," the bounty hunter said as he cracked his knuckles. "Big Blue wants another helping."

Lobo ran up to him and threw a punch. Superman blocked the blow, plus three more. His eyes narrowed as he blasted the bounty hunter with heat vision.

FZZZZZ!

Lobo chuckled. "That tickles!"

Superman was worried about damaging the station as they fought. But Lobo wasn't concerned at all. He grabbed the hero by the uniform and slammed him into the metal wall.

WHAM! YANK!

Lobo pulled Superman out of the giant dent and slammed him into the opposite wall. He used the Man of Steel to make holes all down the corridor.

Superman didn't fight back. He had another plan.

“How badly do you want to save your little friend there?” Lobo asked. “Because I can keep wrecking this place.” He grinned. “And it doesn’t look like it’s in great shape to begin with.”

“Okay, fine,” Superman said. “You win.”

The bounty hunter’s eyes bulged. “Really? No kidding?” He let go of Superman’s uniform.

The Man of Steel smiled. “No, not really.”

Superman held up the small canister he had snatched from Lobo’s belt. He flicked a switch and a plume of gas shot toward the bounty hunter’s face.

TSSSSSSS!

Lobo’s eyes widened as he inhaled the gas. “What a . . . dirty trick,” he said before passing out and crumpling to the floor.

"I learned from the best," Superman said with a smirk.

He stepped over the unconscious bounty hunter and moved toward the Mechanic. The little alien woke up as Superman removed the chain. The Mechanic glanced over at the unconscious bounty hunter. "You did it, Superman," he said. "You saved me."

"Not quite," Superman said. "Now that we're here, let's find out who hired Lobo in the first place."

SHHHHOOP!

A door slid open and two tall, thin aliens stepped through. They had small heads atop long necks with long arms stretching nearly to the floor.

"It is we who hired the bounty hunter to find the Mechanic," said one of the aliens.

The Mechanic hid behind Superman's cape once again.

"We mean you no harm," said the second alien. "We are the Lis-Moorians, and our home, as you can see, is in serious need of repair." The Lis-Moorian lifted one long arm and gestured with a sweeping motion toward the badly damaged corridor.

"Xal Gliknark's reputation is great—but contacting him directly has proved very difficult," the first Lis-Moorian added as she pointed to the Mechanic. "We desperately need his assistance, so we hired Lobo to help us find him."

The tiny alien stepped out from behind Superman. "That's it?" he asked.

The Lis-Moorians nodded. "Only if you agree," they said.

Superman smiled down at the Mechanic. "It looks like you have a chance to help someone now."

A grin stretched across the Mechanic's face as his eyes began to glow. Metal creaked around them as the corridor walls slowly repaired themselves.

Superman's smile faded as deep, groggy laughter echoed in the hallway. Lobo slowly stumbled to his feet. "What did I tell you, Supes?" he said. "The Main Man always delivers."

The first Lis-Moorian handed the bounty hunter a stack of metal bars. "Your payment in full."

Lobo chuckled as he counted them. Then he pushed past Superman as he sauntered toward the air lock.

Superman crossed his arms. "Earth is still off-limits, Lobo."

Lobo waved him away as he reached the hatch. "Don't worry, Supes. The Main Man has no reason to visit that little mud ball of yours." He glanced over his shoulder and grinned. "For now . . ."

Lobo

SPECIES: Czarnian

OCCUPATION: Bounty Hunter

BASE: Mobile

HEIGHT: 7 feet 6 inches

WEIGHT: 640 pounds

EYES: Red

HAIR: Black

POWERS/ABILITIES: Superhuman strength, stamina, and durability. He is also highly skilled at hunting, tracking, and hand-to-hand combat.

BIOGRAPHY:

Lobo is known as the most successful bounty hunter in the entire universe. He always gets his target, even if it means destroying entire planets in pursuit of his prey. In fact, Lobo loves breaking things—and people—so the line of work suits him well. Despite being a self-proclaimed "bad man," Lobo is always true to his word. He will never break his promises, but he does bend them quite often. His employers must choose their words carefully, or they'll end up in a deal they didn't quite bargain for.

- Lobo zooms around from planet to planet atop his trusty, customized hoverbike, the Hog. Since Lobo doesn't need to breathe, he can undergo interstellar travel at super-speed without even wearing a space suit.

- Lobo's accelerated healing abilities allow him to regenerate lost limbs. In fact, Lobo can heal from any injury if he's given enough time.

- Despite his own bad body odor, Lobo has an amazing sense of smell. He is able to sniff out his prey from as far as a galaxy away! He also has the tracking skills of an expert hunter, so hiding from the Main Man is nearly impossible.

BIOGRAPHIES

Author

Michael Anthony Steele has been writing for television, movies, and video games for more than 27 years. He has authored more than 120 books for exciting characters and brands including Batman, Superman, Wonder Woman, Scooby-Doo, LEGO City, Garfield, *Winx Club, Night at the Museum,* and *The Penguins of Madagascar*. Mr. Steele lives on a ranch in Texas, but he enjoys meeting his readers when he visits schools and libraries all across the country. For more information, visit MichaelAnthonySteele.com

Illustrator

Leonel Castellani has worked as a comic artist and illustrator for more than 20 years. Mostly known for his work on licensed art for Warner Bros., DC Comics, Disney, Marvel Entertainment, and Cartoon Network, Leonel has also built a career as a conceptual designer and storyboard artist for video games, movies, and TV. In addition to drawing, Leonel also likes to sculpt and paint. He currently lives in La Plata City, Argentina.

GLOSSARY

annihilate (uh-NYE-uh-late)—to destroy something completely

bounty hunter (BOUN-tee HUN-tur)—someone who tracks and captures others for money

bystander (BYE-stan-dur)—someone who is at a place where something happens to someone else

commander (kuh-MAND-ur)—a person who leads a group of people in a military force

communicator (kuh-MYOO-nuh-kay-tur)—a device that allows people to talk to each other over great distances

derrick (DER-ik)—a tall framework that holds the machines used to drill oil wells

intelligence (in-TEL-uh-jenss)—the ability to learn and understand information

invincible (in-VIN-suh-buhl)—unable to be beaten or defeated

projectile (pruh-JEK-tuhl)—an object, such as a bullet or missile, that is thrown or shot through the air or space

reputation (rep-yuh-TAY-shuhn)—a person's character as judged by other people

unconscious (uhn-KON-shuhss)—not aware; not able to see, feel, or think

DISCUSSION QUESTIONS

1. Superman decides to help the Mechanic without really knowing why Lobo is hunting him. Do you think that was the right decision? Explain your answer.

2. Green Lantern swoops in to help Superman with the standoff in space. Do you think the Man of Steel could have controlled the situation without Green Lantern's help? Why or why not?

3. At the end of the story, we learn the real reason Lobo was hunting the Mechanic. How did that reason change your view of the bounty hunter?

WRITING PROMPTS

1. The Mechanic can build giant creatures out of machines. What would you build if you had his power? Write a paragraph describing your creation. Then draw a picture of it.

2. Superman uses many of his superpowers to battle Lobo. Which power would you like to have most? Write a short story about how you would use that power to help others.

3. The story ends with Superman telling Lobo never to return to Earth. The bounty hunter says he won't "for now." Write a new chapter in which Lobo does return to Earth. Describe how Superman deals with the Main Man a second time.

LOOK FOR MORE

DC SUPER HERO ADVENTURES

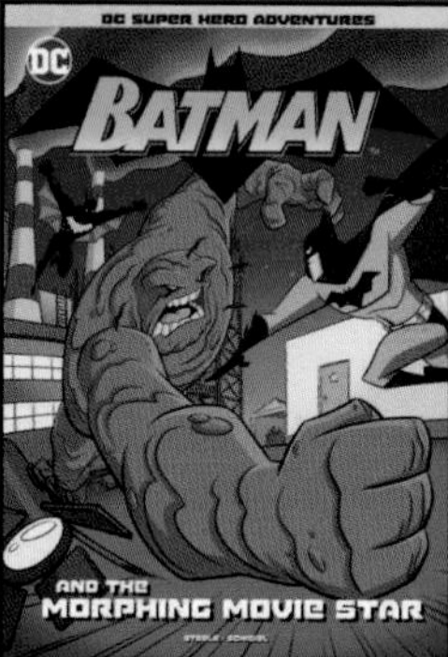

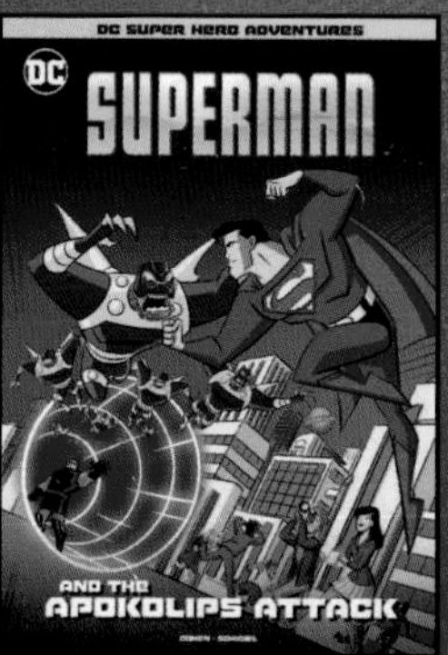

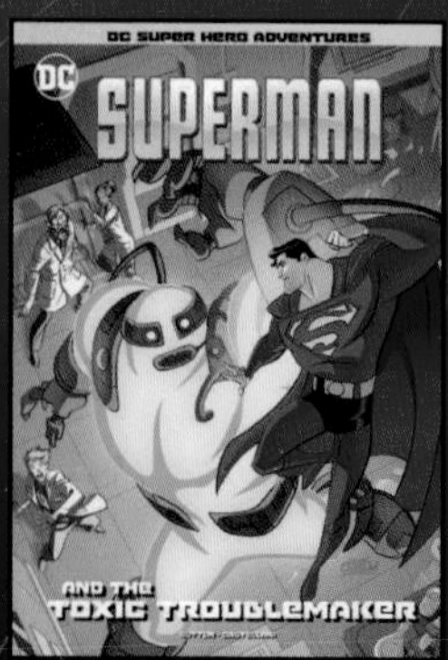

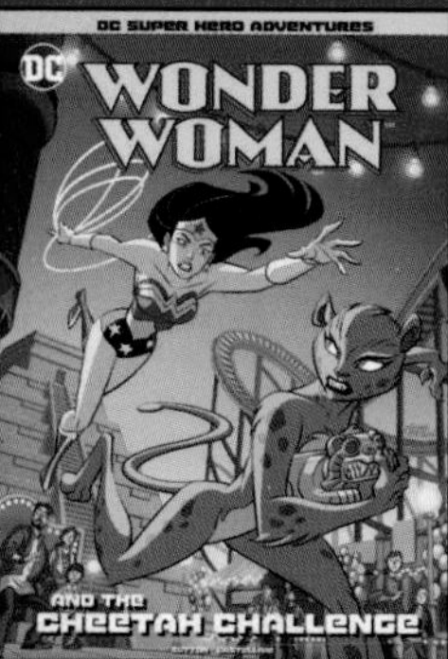